Broken SERIES
BOOK THREE

# Broken promises

NEW YORK TIMES & USA TODAY BESTSELLING AUTHOR
# KELLY ELLIOTT

Copyright © 2014, 2016 by Kelly Elliott
Published by K. Elliott Enterprises

Cover design by Sara Eirew Photographer
Cover photo by Shannon Cain
http://photographybyshannoncain.com
Editor: Emily Anderson with Yellow Bird Editors
Interior Designer: Julie Titus with JT Formatting

First Edition: November 2014
Library of Congress Cataloging-in-Publication Data
Broken Promises (Broken Series, Book 3) – 1st ed
ISBN-13: 978-0990321088

*For exclusive releases and giveaways signup for Kelly's newsletter at*
www.kellyelliottauthor.com

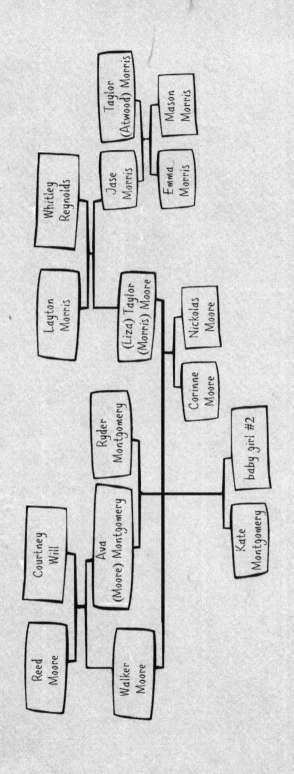

# One

## Liza/Taylor

Staring out the window, I dragged in a long, deep breath as I spun my ring around my finger. I couldn't believe college was over. I closed my eyes and pushed down the same uneasy feeling I'd been pushing down every time I headed home for the last three and half years.

With my eyes closed, I was brought back to that day in the barn when I gave Walker a piece of my heart.

*The last people from the party filed out of the barn and I watched as Walker and Jase said good-bye to their friends. When Walker turned and smiled at me, my heart stopped. I reminded myself that Walker was just a friend. My best friend, but nothing more. I looked over toward Ava and her best friend, Cindy before glancing back at Walker and Jase. Walker had been my best friend since I could remember. Our parents were best friends, so we were always together. Family vacations, birthdays, holidays—whatever*

*we did, our families did it together. At age six, Walker had vowed that he would always protect Ava and me. We were his whole world, and no one would ever hurt his sisters.*

*The problem was, Ava was his sister, and I was the best friend who'd been in love with him since the day he made that promise.*

*Jase laughed and asked me, "How do you think it went?"*

*I shook my head and said, "If Mom and Dad find out that you threw Walker and me a going away party in their barn, they're going to be pissed."*

*Jase and Ava both laughed.*

*"Please. I've heard all of Uncle Layton's pontoon party stories. One little barn party is nothing," Ava said.*

*Jase winked at Ava. "A girl after my own heart."*

*Ava gave Jase the finger and turned to head out of the barn. "Cindy and I are heading home, Liza. See you in a few," she called over her shoulder.*

*Everyone had been calling me Liza since I was little, even though my first name was Taylor. It was short for Elizabeth, my middle name.*

*Jase watched Ava leave the barn and he laughed. "Good thing I have a girlfriend." He shook Walker's hand, then kissed me on the cheek. "Love you, sis," he whispered.*

*"Watch it," Walker said. "Ava is still my baby sister, Jase."*

*Jase laughed and walked out of the barn, saying, "I threw the party. Y'all clean up."*

*I stood and called out, "Jase Morris! You'd better get your ass back in here right now and help!"*

*Walker shook his head. "Come on. By the time you talk him into helping, we can have the whole place cleaned up."*

*As Walker and I cleaned up the empty cups and trash, we talked about college. Walker was going to Texas A&M to major in biological and agricultural engineering. I was going to Baylor University and getting my degree in education. My dream was to be an elementary school teacher right here in Llano.*

*"Are you still thinking of minoring in horticulture?" I asked as I threw the last empty cup away. I wiped my sticky hands on my pants.*

*Jase had promised no alcohol, but I was pretty sure that some people had snuck some in. The evidence was all over my hands.*

*Walker chuckled. "I'm not sure. I think I'll be too busy with my major, and my dad says he doesn't want me pushing it."*

*I rinsed off my hands in the sink at the end of the barn, then made my way over to a bunch of hay bales. I flopped down and giggled.*

*"I think you probably know just as much as the teachers anyway," I said, "with what all you've learned from your dad."*

*He nodded. "Yeah. My main goal is to help my dad and Layton out on the ranch. I'm itching to get into the racehorse world, but my damn dad won't even let me go to the races."*

*I threw my head back and laughed. As I pulled my knees up to my chest, I looked at Walker and shook my head. "You don't think it has anything to do with the fact that he caught you getting people to place bets on the horses, do you?"*

*Walker gave me that smile that had been melting my heart for years as he sat next to me. I'd learned to cover up my true feelings for him, but he still did things to my insides.*

*"Liza, can I ask you something?"*

*I shrugged and said, "Of course you can. You never have to ask that."*

*He looked out the barn door. "Why haven't you ever dated anyone for very long?"*

*His question totally caught me off guard, and I dropped my legs and sat up, clearing my throat. "Um...I don't know. I just want to be with that one person who...who, um..."*

*Walker was still staring off in the distance as he said, "Makes your heart stop beating?" he barely said.*

*I stared at him. "Yes."*

*"I want the type of love that takes my breath away," Walker said as he turned and looked into my eyes.*

*"Yeah. Me, too," I whispered as I looked away. "What about you? Never found that one girl who makes your heart stop?" I asked as I bumped his shoulder with mine.*

*When he took my hand, I sucked in a breath and tried to contain the crazy feeling zipping through my body. As our eyes met, something happened. Something changed between us, and my heart slammed against my chest.*

*Walker stood, pulled me up, and brought me close. When he placed his finger on my chin, his eyes landed on my lips, and I fought to hold in a moan. He leaned down and brushed his lips against mine. We shared that first kiss, slow, yet full of passion. Our tongues danced, and we both moaned as Walker pulled me against his body.*

*When he pulled his lips away, he whispered, "Promise me something." I swallowed hard and whispered back, "Anything." Walker looked into my eyes and smiled. "Wait for me, Liza."*

*I smiled. "Okay."*

*"Say it, Liza," Walker said.*

*I tried desperately to ignore the feeling of him pressing himself into me as I said, "I promise, Walker, I'll wait for you."*

"Liza? Liza, are you listening to me?" Keith asked as he nudged my leg.

I shook my head and chuckled. "Sorry, I was just thinking."

"Aww, my deep thinker. Always lost in thought. What were you thinking about this time? A wedding perhaps?"

Keith had asked me to marry him last December when I went home with him to meet his family. It was the first Christmas I wasn't home with my own family. And the first Christmas I hadn't seen Walker. I chewed on my lip, like I always did. It was a nervous habit I'd picked up years ago, and it drove my father crazy.

"Um…just wondering what this summer will hold for me," I said. "For us,"

Keith shook his head and sighed. "Liza, when are you going to give me an answer? I feel like I've been pretty damn patient considering the fact that you turned me down in front of my entire family."

I looked out the window. Keith and I had been dating since the spring semester of our freshman year. Walker and I had decided over Christmas that year that there was no way we could make a relationship work when we were going to separate schools. It took Walker until the next year to start dating. I'd always felt guilty that I'd moved on faster.

"You told me I had until the end of the summer, Keith. You prom-

4

ised."

Keith grabbed my hand and kissed the back of it. I couldn't help but smile when I looked at him. Keith and I met through a mutual friend at a party. The moment I looked into his hazel eyes I longed to run my fingers through his messy dark blond hair. He was just under six feet tall and played soccer. His body was amazing. I longed to unbuckle my seatbelt and kiss him

I closed my eyes and pushed my wandering thoughts away.

"I know I told you that, and I'm sorry, Liza," he said. "I just don't understand why this is so hard for you. You either want to marry me or you don't."

I inhaled and let my breath out slowly. We'd been having this argument since Christmas Eve. "Keith, all I've ever wanted is to teach elementary school in Llano. It's hard to just walk away from a dream."

He let go of my hand and ran his fingers through his hair. "It shouldn't be hard if you're doing it for love. You can teach in Dallas, baby. There are *hundreds* of schools. You want more space, we'll move to the suburbs. I'll move where ever you want to go."

I was about to say Llano when he raised an eyebrow.

"Except for hicktown," he said.

I rolled my eyes. "I wish you wouldn't call it that. Llano is my hometown, Keith. I love it there. My family and friends are there."

"Maybe it's time to make new friends, and belong to another family."

"Are you asking me to give up my family now?" I asked, glaring.

He looked at me with a stunned look. "What? No. Of course not, Liza. You know what I meant. You'll have my family in Dallas. Your new family."

I looked out the front window. Keith was pulling into the Austin airport. I placed my hand on my stomach, trying to settle my nerves. I wasn't sure if I was nervous about Keith leaving for the summer or if I was nervous about seeing Walker. It had been a year since we'd seen each other. He'd gone to his girlfriend's parents' ranch over Thanksgiving last year, and then at Christmas I was at Keith's parents' house in Dallas.

I pushed open the door to my Toyota Camry. I stepped into the sun and closed my eyes as I felt the heat on my face. I couldn't wait to get home and go down to our dock on the lake and just sit in peace. And think.

"You think too much, Liza." Keith said, kissing the tip of my nose. I opened my eyes and smiled weakly.

"What makes you think I was thinking?" I asked as I wrapped my arms around his waist. He laughed and looked into my blue eyes. "Baby, you're always thinking about something. You need to give your brain the summer off." He pulled back and met my gaze. "Please, Liza. Just wear the ring. I don't want an answer until I get back."

"Keith, you know I love you and—"

"For me, Liza. Please wear the ring."

I swallowed and pulled my hand out of my pocket, looking at the ring I was already wearing. Walker had given it to me before we left for college. It was two hearts intertwined. Keith had asked me about the ring shortly after we started dating. I told him the truth: It was from my best friend and it meant a lot to me. I constantly played with it when something was bothering me or I was deep in thought.

Keith reached into his pocket and pulled out the engagement ring he'd bought. My hand shook as Keith lifted my hand. My heart pounded as Keith slipped Walker's ring off my finger. "Can we put this on your necklace for now? I don't think Walker would mind, do you?"

Tears were building in my eyes. I felt so guilty for wearing Walker's ring while dating Keith. I reached up, unclasped my necklace, and held it while Keith dropped the silver ring onto the chain. I clasped it back on my neck, my hands shaking. Keith opened the box and took out the way-too-extravagant diamond ring. He put the red velvet box away in his front pocket and reached for my left hand. I watched as he slipped the ring onto my finger. A single tear slipped from my eye and traveled down my cheek. Keith gently wiped my tear away.

"Please tell me that is a happy tear, Liza," he said.

I nodded and smiled when he leaned down for a gentle kiss.

He pulled back slightly and said, "I have to go, but I really don't want to go. I want to wrap myself around your body and make love to you."

My stomach took a sharp dip. Keith was so romantic and such a sweet, gentle lover. But sometimes I just wanted…more. I wanted passion. Raw passion. I wanted him to look at me like he couldn't wait to have me. Like he wanted me and only me.

He pulled me into his arms. "Thank you for putting it on, baby. I'm going to miss you so damn much. God, Liza I don't want to leave."

I held onto him and closed my eyes. My emotions were all over the place. One minute I wanted to tell him not to leave—that I would marry him tomorrow if he wanted. The next, I was confused as hell about the feelings I still had for Walker.

Keith pulled back. I slid my hands into my back pockets.

"I love you, Liza," he said. "I'll see you August twenty-fourth."

I nodded as I wiped away my tears. "Be careful," I said. "Tell your dad I said 'Hi' and that I miss him." I said as Keith picked up his suitcases. Keith and his father, Tom, where going hiking along the Appalachian Trail together this summer. They'd been planning the trip for years. The moment Keith graduated, they wanted to spend a few months together, just the two of them. I knew how much this meant to Keith, especially since his father beat cancer two years ago.

Keith took a few steps back and gave me that sweet smile of his. "I'll text or call when I get a signal."

I sniffled and said, "Okay. Be careful."

"Always, baby. I love you and I can't wait to get home and make you my wife." He quickly turned away before I could even say anything.

I watched him walk into the airport. When I could no longer see him, I turned and got back into my car, pulling in a deep breath. I rested my head on the seatback. I was going to miss him. I lifted up my hand and looked at the ring, wondering if I could marry Keith, if I even wanted to. I thought I did, but I wasn't so sure. Shaking my head, I let out a frustrated sigh. *What the hell is wrong with me?* I needed to come to terms with the idea of following my dreams in Dallas, with Keith.

I looked forward and pulled out my phone and texted Jase.

**Me**: *Hey.*
**Jase**: *Hey, big sis. Are you on your way home?*
**Me**: *Yep. Just dropped off Keith and will be there in a few hours. My car is packed down with stuff.*
**Jase**: *Mom and dad have a surprise party planned for you.*
**Me**: *Oh, shit. No.*
**Jase**: *Yep. Dad even bought something to try to persuade you to stay in Llano.*

"Great. Just what I need, my father butting in and making me more confused," I said to myself as I started the car. I looked down at my phone and sent my brother a text.

**Me**: *Tell dad he can't sway me, one way or the other. Then tell him I love him. Who all is there?*
**Jase**: *Just us, big sis. No one loves you enough to show up.*

I laughed and shook my head as I tossed my phone to the side. When I heard my phone beep, I took one last look at it. My heart rate picked up when I read Jase's last text.

**Jase**: *Just kidding. Walker just showed up.*

# Two

## Walker

I took a deep breath as I looked at Liza's house. I hadn't seen her since last summer, and it had only been for five minutes. Jessica had been with me, and when I'd tried to talk to Liza, it had been awkward as hell. She didn't notice me looking at her finger and seeing the ring I'd given her before we left for college. I was shocked that she still wore it. She'd been dating her rich asshole boyfriend for three years or so. She seemed happy.

I stepped out of my truck and was about to make my way to the front door when I remembered that, last time I walked through that door, I'd had every intention of telling Liza how much I still thought about her. I'd wanted to take her in my arms and tell her how I still felt.

"Walker!"

I turned to see Ava running toward me. I smiled and held out my arms, ready for a full force blow when she threw her body into mine. And that's exactly what she did. I was almost knocked backwards as I laughed. "Why hello there, Ava Grace."

I set her down and she hit me on the shoulder. "Don't call me that. I hate it. Just Ava." She gave me a once-over and glanced into the truck before asking, "No Jessica?"

I shook my head. "Not this time."

Ava sighed. "Bummer. I was really hoping to pick her brain about France."

Ava took my hand as we made our way up to the front door of the Morris' house. "So is Jessica excited about moving to the ranch?"

"I think so," I said, shrugging. "She's in Europe with her mother and grandmother right now. They're touring."

My sister was going to be over the moon when she realized that she'd have my full attention all summer. I usually came home, worked on the ranch, and then drove into Austin to be with Jessica.

Ava's eyes lit up. "Really? I have you all to myself?"

I chuckled and nodded. "At least until August twenty-sixth."

Ava screamed as she flew into my arms. The door flew open and I turned to see Jase there, smiling. He seemed to be finishing up a text. When he looked back up he had a shit-eating grin on his face.

"What's up bro?" I asked, giving him a quick handshake.

"Where's your hot girlfriend?"

Ava pushed past Jase and called out over her shoulder, "She's touring Europe."

Jase threw his head back and laughed, slapping me on the shoulder. "Damn, dude. Liza's gonna be stoked."

I looked at him, shocked. "What? Why?"

Jase smiled and said, "Cause the gang is back together."

I nodded, "Oh yeah. Right."

I looked up and finally noticed the giant sign. *Congratulations Taylor and Walker.*

"She's gonna be pissed," I whispered.

Jase looked at the sign and shrugged. "Dude, I told my mom not to use Taylor, to use Liza," Jase said as he looked around for his mom. "Mom says they accidentally put Taylor and by the time she noticed, it was too late to fix it."

Layton and my father both rounded the corner. My father's smile lit up his face when he saw me. He held out his hand as I reached for it. "Dad," I said with a smile. I reached my hand out for Layton's. "Sir, how are you?" I asked with a nod. I'd known Layton forever, since he was Jase and Liza's father, but I couldn't help but call him "sir."

Layton gave me a once-over. "Well, I'm glad to see you kept in shape, Walker. I'm going to put your ass to work starting tomorrow morning. There's a fence that needs mending in the front pasture over by Mimi and Frank's place."

"Yes, sir. I'm ready to get to work." I said.

My father gave me a look and motioned for me to join him outside. Before I turned to follow him through the house and out the back door, though, I said, "Layton, sir. Do you have a Sharpie I can use? The kind with the thick, bold tip?"

Layton nodded. "Yeah, I've got one."

"Dad, one second while I fix something."

Layton returned from his office with a fat Sharpie. I grabbed a chair and stood on it to reach the sign. I drew an X through Taylor and wrote Liza in huge letters. Everyone started laughing. I jumped down and handed the Sharpie back to Layton and followed my father through the kitchen and to the back porch.

"Where's Mom?" I asked.

My father headed down the steps. "Courtney's checking on Mimi and Frank. They're getting older, but insist on living in that giant ranch house all alone."

We walked down to the main barn in silence. The moment we stepped into the barn, I was thrown back to the night I'd kissed Liza. I shook my head and attempted to push the memory away.

"So Jessica's on her way to Europe?" My father asked as he took a seat.

I let out a tired breath and sat across from him. "Yep. Well, they leave tomorrow."

"Is she excited about moving out here?"

I shrugged. "She said she was. Her parents are pushing for us to get married though."

My father nodded his head slowly. "How do you feel about that?"

"About marrying, Jessica?"

He laughed. "Isn't that who we're talking about?"

"I don't know dad. I mean, I've looked at rings a few times and it just doesn't feel right. I love Jessica. I just don't understand the rush to get married."

He stood up and nodded. "And how does Jessica feel about that? She seemed like a really sweet girl when we met her last summer. Is she okay with waiting?"

I thought back to yesterday when I'd dropped Jessica off at her house after having dinner with her parents.

*"So, do you have a going away present for me?" Jessica asked with her cute little smile.*

*"Ah...I didn't know I was supposed to get you a gift, baby. I'm sorry." Her face dropped and she looked out the window. I placed my finger on her chin and pulled her eyes back to mine. "Jess, I didn't even think about it."*

*Her jaw tightened and I knew it was coming. "I find it funny that you thought to buy your best friend a ring when y'all went off to college, but when your girlfriend is leaving for the whole summer, and returning to live with you on your family's ranch, it doesn't even pop into your head that maybe you should buy her something."*

*I closed my eyes and let out a long, slow breath. "Jesus, Jess. Why do you always bring that damn ring up? I wish I'd never told you about it. What do you want from me?"*

*"A commitment, Walker. Something that tells me you want the same things I want. I want to know that I'm not picking up my entire life and moving out to the country for a man who doesn't want the same things I want."*

*"Jessica, I just don't see why we should rush into getting married just because we graduated."*

*She laughed. "I'm not asking you to marry me tomorrow, Walker. I'm asking you to commit. To give me something."*

*I nodded and looked into her eyes. "I promise, I'll give you what you're asking for."*

*"When?" she asked, raising an eyebrow.*

*I swallowed hard. "By the end of summer."*

*She smiled. "Is that a promise?"*

"Walker?" My father snapped his fingers in my face. "Earth to Walker."

I laughed. "Sorry, Dad. I was thinking of something." Smiling, I slapped his back. "Dad, Jessica and I talked before she left for Europe. I'm planning on asking her to marry me before she moves out to the ranch. That doesn't mean we're gonna rush into a wedding, but she wants a commitment from me and I intend to give her one."

My father smiled and nodded. "That sounds like the young man I raised. We'll go down to the foreman's cabin and show you how Layton and I fixed it up. We added another room so Jessica could have an office. I think you'll both be very pleased."

"I can't wait to see it," I said. "I'll take pictures and send them to her."

My dad led us back up to the house. As we walked, I heard someone pulling up the driveway. I'd parked out front, leaving room for Liza's car in the back by the garage. When I saw her Camry come around the corner I couldn't help but smile as I said, "Looks like Liza's home."

Right behind Liza were Whitley and my mother. The second I saw Liza step out of her car, the wind swept up her long, chestnut hair, I had to catch my breath. *Shit. That hasn't happened to me in a long time. What is the matter with me?*

Whitley and my mother both squealed as Ava came running out the back door screaming. They all tackled Liza and started crying.

"Why do they do that?" I asked.

My father was watching the whole thing play out. "Why do they do what?"

I gestured toward the women. "Scream and cry like that. I mean, I get that Liza hasn't been home in a while, but good lord."

My father shook his head. "Son that is the first of many, many questions you're going to have about women. Almost all of them come down to 'why do they do that?'"

I laughed and followed my father over to Liza's car. Layton was hugging her and Jase was waiting for his turn. As much as he tried to be a badass, he loved his sister—and mine. There was nothing he wouldn't do for either of them.

13

Liza turned around and the smile on her face about dropped me to my knees. *Holy shit.* Her hair was escaping from a loose bun on top of her head, despite a bandana wrapped around her head. My eyes traveled up and down her body as I took in the jean shorts, cowboy boots and pink T-shirt. Her smile faded briefly when she saw me, but she quickly brought it back when my father hugged her.

"My gosh, you're not my little Liza who use to beg me to take her fishing every Saturday on the pontoon boat."

Liza laughed. "I'm still that girl, just a little older. I still want to go fishing, Reed."

My father took a step back and I approached Liza. I hadn't felt this happy in a long time. I glanced at something hanging around her neck. When I saw that it was the ring I'd given her, I looked down to her left hand. That's when I saw the giant-ass engagement ring. I stopped dead in my tracks. Liza chuckled nervously and gave me a quick hug.

"Hey, you. Oh my gosh it's been what? A year?"

I couldn't pull my eyes from the ring. *Liza was engaged?* When I finally met her gaze, she glanced briefly at her ring before putting her hand in her pocket.

"Um…how have you been?" she asked.

"You're engaged?" I blurted. Her smile dropped and she squinted her left eye at me, just like she always did when she was agitated.

"What did you say, Walker?" Whitley asked.

That's when I noticed Liza biting her lip. I realized she didn't want anyone to know she was engaged. But why?

"I um," I said "Just, wow, it's been a long time since we've seen each other."

Liza let out the breath she was holding and smiled weakly at me.

I smiled back before starting back toward the barn.

"Walker?" she called after me.

I just kept walking. It felt like all of the air had been pulled from my lungs as I desperately attempted to drag in air. *She'd moved on—again.*

# Three

## Liza

I watched as Walker walked toward the barn. My first instinct was to go after him. Instead, I plastered on a fake-ass smile for everyone.

My mother pulled me in for another hug. "I'm so glad you're home," she whispered into my ear.

I held her tighter. "Me too, Mom. Me too."

My father clapped his hands said, "Let's head back in and eat some barbecue ribs, shall we?"

I looked back toward the barn as Jase and Walker both walked through the barn doors. I turned to my father who gave me a funny look, then winked.

Walking into the kitchen, I instantly felt relaxed. I loved being home. I loved our ranch, the river, the cows, the horses. I loved everything about this place. My mother and Courtney were getting everything ready for us to sit and have a feast. Ava was bouncing around, talking a mile a minute about how she only had one year of college left. Her degree was in design, and she would be interning this summer at design firm in Austin.

"Liza, how is Keith?" Courtney asked as Reed wrapped his arms around her.

I smiled at their display of affection. Walker and Ava were just like their parents. Ava was the spitting image of her Courtney. Walker was a younger version of Reed. When I'd seen Walker earlier, it took everything out of me to keep my jaw from dropping. Walker had clearly been working out. He was bigger than he was last summer. His messy brown hair always looked like he'd just run his hands through it after a shower. When my eyes were searching his body, I'd noticed a piece of a tattoo on his right arm, peeking out from his T-shirt. His blue eyes had pierced mine, demanding my attention, like always.

The moment he'd noticed the ring on my finger, I'd seen the hurt in his eyes. It had just about gutted me. I can't believe I was so stupid—I'd meant to take it off. My phone buzzed in my pocket and I pulled it out.

**Keith**: *I just landed. Are you home?*
**Me**: *Yep! Just got here a bit ago.*
**Keith**: *Have you told your folks the news?*
**Me**: *News??*
**Keith**: *Yes, Liza. Our engagement!*

I rolled my eyes and looked around. Everyone was busy talking so I walked out into the living room.

**Me**: *I haven't officially said yes yet.*
**Keith**: *You're wearing the ring though, right?*

I pulled my hand up and looked at the massive oval-cut diamond on my finger. I tried to take a deep, cleansing breath. I need to take this massive thing off.

**Me**: *Yes. But, Keith, you gave me until the end of summer. Remember?*

Then I heard a scream. My mother came running toward me. "Taylor Elizabeth Morris! Why didn't you tell us?"

I gave her a confused look and laughed. "What are you talking about, Mom?"

I caught my mother staring at my hand, and I instantly spun the ring around and attempted to put my hand in my pocket. But she was quick, grabbing my arm and pulling it out. She gasped when she saw the ring. *Shit. Shit. Shit.*

"Liza," My mother implored. "Why in the world didn't you tell us that Keith asked you to marry him at Christmas?"

I tried to talk, but nothing came out—I was too surprised.

How in the world did my mother know that Keith asked me to marry him last Christmas? I tried to clear my head, but now Ava was grabbing my hand and Courtney was next in line.

"It's beautiful!" Ava said. "Oh, wow. That thing must have cost him a fortune."

"Ava Grace, that is just rude. Try to filter yourself—even if I don't," Courtney said, holding my hand to examine the ring.

My mother placed her hands on her hips. "Well?"

"Um, well, what?" I said as I chewed on my lip. I could feel it swelling—I was abusing the hell out of it.

Mom shook her head. "I want to know why I had to hear it from Keith."

"Hear what from Keith? Mom, you're really confusing me." My phone buzzed in my hand and I glanced down to see Keith's text. All I saw on the screen was "Sorry."

I opened the message. I could feel the anger building the moment I read his text.

**Keith**: *Sorry. I texted your mom and asked if she was excited and whether she'd seen the ring yet.*

I tried to smile at my mother. That's when I saw the sign behind her. "Taylor" was crossed out with "Liza" written above it. I instantly knew who'd done it. *Walker.*

"Liza? What are you thinking about? Why didn't you tell us about the engagement?" My mother said as my father came in.

"What engagement?" he asked.

Ava started jumping. "Liza is engaged! She's getting married."

My father turned quickly. "What? Liza, is that true?"

My heart was beating faster than ever. I wasn't sure if I was pissed at

Keith or upset with myself.

I placed my hand on my temple. "Wait. Give me a second here." Ava was still bouncing around. "Ava! Cut it out!" I yelled. She instantly stopped and stared at me.

I glanced at my mother who now looked very concerned. My father just seemed confused as hell. Before I could stop myself, I blurted, "I'm not engaged!"

Everyone was staring at the engagement ring on my finger. When I saw blue eyes gazing at me from the door, I sucked in a breath. Then my phone rang. I glanced down—it was Keith. I was too angry to talk to him right now.

My mother cleared her throat, waiting for an explanation.

I took a deep breath and said, "I mean. I'm not...I haven't said yes...yet."

I risked a look at Walker, who just stared back at me. Then he checked his phone. As he walked away, I heard him say, "Hey, Jess...are you getting ready to leave?"

I'd wanted to grill Ava, to see if Walker was still dating Jessica. I guess I didn't have to. I tried desperately to quell the jealous feelings that ran rampant in me.

I tried to laugh. "I mean, I told Keith I wanted to wait until after college to make my decision."

"Smart girl," My father said. "I knew I raised you right."

I giggled nervously as I glanced back over to Walker. He was still standing in the corner, talking on the phone. He was smiling when I read his lips saying, "I love you."

He pulled the phone away and must have hung up. He looked directly at me, but I looked away, continuing to explain the engagement thing to my parents.

"I, um...I told him I would for sure give him my answer by the time he came back from his hiking trip with his dad. He uh...well, he asked me to wear the ring, so..." I held it up and tried to laugh before I dropped my hand and shrugged.

Ava pulled me in for a hug. "Well, I know that you wouldn't have put it on if you didn't think your answer would be 'yes.'"

I swallowed as I peeked over to Walker. He gave me a weak smile.

"Well," I said, "we still have some things to talk about so…" I trailed off as I saw the look on my mother's face—it was like she could see the internal struggle going on in my head. "Anyway," I said. "I'm starved. Are those ribs done yet?"

Everyone dispersed. Jase and Walker headed into the den and mentioned something about playing a game of pool. We'd always loved to play pool. Walker had taught me how to play and Jase hated that I constantly beat him.

"After dinner boys," Courtney called. "Let's eat!"

Courtney carried a giant bowl of potato salad to the table and I was more than happy to help out. Anything to turn the conversation away from the ring.

I stood at the kitchen sink staring out the window as I dried off a plate. I felt someone pull the plate from my hand and turned to see my mother. She was so beautiful, like always. Her hair was pulled up in a simple ponytail and her blue eyes sparkled as she looked into mine.

"Follow your heart," she whispered. "I promise, it will always lead you down the right path."

I felt the tears building in my eyes. "Mom," I whispered as she took me into her arms. I fought like hell to hold my tears back as she held me. I'd missed her so much. *Did I really want to leave all of this? Leave my family?* I pulled back and wiped a tear away. "Thanks, Mom."

"I'm always here to talk, sweetheart. Please know that." She pushed a stray strand of hair back and behind me ear.

I nodded. "I know that, Mom."

She smiled said, "Now go play pool and show your brother Jase how it's done."

I laughed as I set the towel down and made my way through the house to the den. When I walked in, Ava and Jase were arguing about some rule.

"Ava, if an 8 ball is knocked to the floor, it's a loss. Period." Jase said.

Ava stood firm with her hands on her hips. "I don't think so, Jase. Stop trying to kick me out of the game."

Jase threw his hands up and sighed in frustration.

When I looked to my right, I saw Walker. He was leaning against the wall watching Ava and Jase fight. He was wearing that drop-dead gorgeous smile of his. He had on a light blue T-shirt that made his chest look massive and his biceps even bigger. I licked my lips when I saw the tattoo again. I checked out his pants—Wranglers. Tight Wranglers. I smiled when I noticed he was wearing the same boots he'd always worn when he worked on the ranch. I imagined what it would feel like to have his lips against mine again. *Would that same spark still be there? Would it be lost because he was in love with Jessica? And I was with Keith.*

Walker saw me and pushed off against the wall. I touched the ring that was still on my necklace. Walker's smile wavered for a moment.

"You don't have to keep that ring if you don't want it," he said.

My heart dropped. I wanted to tell him I hadn't taken it off since the day he'd given it to me. Not until today. "Of course I want it," I said. "You gave it to me."

He smiled, then turned to Ava and Jase. "All right I've had enough," he said. "Ava, Jase is right. Let's just rack 'em up and start a new game."

Ava rolled her eyes and made a sour face at Jase. "Ugh, when are you going to Italy?"

He laughed. "You know you're gonna miss me," he said as he mussed up Ava's hair.

She pushed his hand away and said, "Yeah, don't count on it, ass wipe. If I had to push the airplane down the runway to get you out of here, I'd do it."

I giggled and reached for a pool cue. Jase and Ava acted so much like brother and sister. I asked Ava once if she'd ever had feelings for Jase, and she told me they'd once snuck behind the bleachers to make out. When I asked her what happened, she said they'd both ended up laughing and had spent the rest of the night talking about the future.

We'd grown up together, but all had different plans. Ava wanted to be in design and planned to develop her own clothing line. Wedding couture was her dream. Jase loved ranching. It was in his blood, for sure. He planned to return to Llano after next summer's trip to Italy to help our father with the ranch. Walker had more love for the racehorse side of the business and was planning a trip to Kentucky with our fathers in a few weeks.

"So are you looking forward to Italy, Jase?" I asked.

I racked the balls and got ready to start and a new game. I smiled when I noticed Walker's eyes moving over my body. After finding out Walker was home, I'd pulled over and changed into my favorite boots and shorts. Keith didn't like me dressing this way. He preferred to see me in dresses. He thought boots and shorts together were "trampy."

I hit the cue ball and smiled when I sunk four balls.

"Shit," Jase said. "I thought maybe you'd be rusty and we'd have an edge."

I held up my cue and blew on the end. "I'm on fire tonight, little brother. Sit back and see how it's done."

Jase sat down on a stool and rolled his eyes.

Five games later, Jase put up his pool cue. "This is bullshit. I'm heading out. Y'all coming?"

Ava jumped up. "Where are we going?"

Jase looked around. "Luckenbach?"

I smiled. It had been so long since I'd gone out. I just wanted to dance and have a good time. "Let me change and I'm so there," I said.

But Walker was texting someone. The smile on his face made my heart ache. I cleared my throat and tried to sound like I didn't care. "You in or out?"

He looked up. "What? I'm sorry. What are y'all talking about?"

Jase laughed, "Dude if you weren't sexting with your damn girlfriend you'd know. We're heading to Luckenbach. Get a bit of dancing in. Do you need to ask your woman?"

Walker grimaced as he stood, shoving Jase. "Fuck off. You wish you *had* a woman."

Jase chuckled. "Dude, please. I can get a piece of ass anytime I want."

I heard my mother clear her throat.

Jase's face turned bright red. He turned to her and said, "Mom, you know I'm just talking shit."

My mother rolled her eyes. "Oh, I know you are, son. I know you are," she said, eliciting laughs from the group. "Y'all be careful. I want a designated driver."

I looked back at Walker. He was staring at me. "I'll volunteer," he

21

said, not taking his eyes off of me. "I bet Liza wants to celebrate her engagement."

My jaw dropped. I was pissed. I cocked my head as I smiled at Walker. "You know, that sounds like a good idea. I think a night of celebrating is just what I need."

Walker pushed off the wall, coming closer. "Too bad your fiancé can't join the fun." He walked away, calling out, "Come on, Ava. We'll pick y'all up in thirty minutes."

"Thirty minutes? Hell, I need at least an hour to get ready," Ava said as she followed Walker out of the den.

My mother winked and said, "Do I sense a bit of tension between you and Walker?"

Jase pushed by and kissed my mother on the cheek before turning to me. "When isn't there tension between the two of them?" he said.

I giggled nervously and kissed my mother on the cheek. "Nah. I think we just haven't seen each other in so long. We're trying to get back into the swing of things."

She nodded and said, "I was hoping we could talk tomorrow."

"Of course, Mom. Maybe we can go for a ride and picnic by the river? I'm dying to get my feet in that water!"

"Sounds like a plan, Liza. Have fun tonight."

As I made my way up to my room, I looked down at my engagement ring. I walked over to my dresser, pulled the ring off my finger, and opened my jewelry box. I set the ring inside and closed the lid. Then I unclasped my necklace and took Walker's ring off of it. I set it on the dresser with my necklace and closed my eyes. If I wanted to move on with my future, I needed to leave the past behind.

I pulled out my phone and flopped onto my bed. The moment I heard Keith's voice, I wanted to lay into him for what he'd done. I took a deep breath and said, "Hey."

"Hey, baby. Listen, I'm so sorry I did that to you, Liza. You asked for the summer, and I didn't abide by the rules. Do you hate me?"

"No, of course not. But I'm not going to lie and say I wasn't pissed off."

"I love you, Liza."

I closed my eyes. When I opened them, a single tear escaped. I was so confused. I loved Keith. But did I want to leave everything and everyone I knew behind to marry him? I wasn't sure yet.

"I love you, too," I said. "Are y'all on your way?"

Keith laughed. "Yeah. Road trip and hiking trip with my old man. Fun times ahead."

I laughed and sat up. "I better run. We're all going out dancing tonight."

Silence. I braced myself for what was about to come.

"Walker going?" Keith asked.

I sighed. "Keith, when are you going to move past this?"

"When you stop wearing the damn ring he gave you. My ring should be on your finger. Not his."

I looked down and instantly felt guilty. I walked over to my jewelry box and took out the engagement ring. I slipped it on my finger, then picked up Walker's double heart ring.

"I'm not doing this with you again. It's getting old."

I heard Keith take a deep breath. "I'm sorry, Liza. I'm really trying. I won't bring it up again. But promise that you'll keep my ring on. I want you to think of me every time you see it."

Slipping Walker's ring back onto the necklace I placed it on the dresser. "Thank you for letting it go. I promise, I'll keep the ring on. But I need to get going. Text or call me when y'all stop for the night."

"All right, baby. I love you."

I smiled at the ring on my finger. "I am wearing it, Keith. And I love you, too."

"Night, baby."

"Night," I said.

I hung up and let out a sigh. *I love Keith. I want a future with him. Didn't I?*

# Four

## Walker

I watched from the bar as Liza danced with some cowboy to Florida Georgia's "This is How We Roll." I turned away and motioned for another Coke.

The bartender smiled. "You're being kind of boring, cowboy," she said as she slid a shot in front of me.

I raised an eyebrow at her. She was cute—long blonde hair and sultry hazel eyes.

I pushed the drink back and winked. "I'm driving tonight and I'm also taken."

She pouted and poured me another Coke and drank the shot.

I saw my sister Ava dancing with some guy. The way his hands were all over her made me want to punch him in the nuts. But Ava had already given me a talk, telling me not to even look at her. She wanted to have fun—if that meant some flirting and a few guys coping a feel, I guess that was her business.

The song ended and Liza came up to the bar. She was well on her way to being drunk, if she wasn't already. She grabbed my Coke and drank it down in one gulp. She put the glass down and made a face.

"Yuck. That's just a Coke."

I nodded. "Um, yeah. Designated driver here, remember?"

She rolled her eyes and called for the bartender. The blonde came over and eyed Liza—she probably thought Liza was my girlfriend.

"I'll take a fireball," Liza said. "No! I'll take two!"

The bartender nodded, looking at me, as if for permission. But if this is what Liza needed to do to feel good, who was I to stop her?

When the shots were placed in front of Liza, I slid the money to the bartender. She winked and said, "You might be getting lucky tonight."

I laughed and said, "I don't think so."

Liza downed one shot and then the next. She let out a little yelp and licked her lips. When she looked at me, my dick jumped. *Fuck. Don't think about her that way, Walker. You have Jessica. She loves you and wants a future with you.*

"Will you dance with me, Walker?" Liza asked, an innocent smile playing on her lips.

They'd been playing nothing but fast songs all night. I nodded, took her hand, and led her to the dance floor. The moment I turned to face her, the song changed. "Glass" by Thompson Square began playing. I swallowed hard and my heart instantly slammed. A slow song meant holding Liza close, pressed up against me. She came closer and I took her in my arms. As we danced, her smell brought me back to those moments we'd spent alone together before leaving for college. I'd often wondered if we'd made the right choice in not sleeping together. Maybe if we had, we'd have fought harder to make things work between us.

I leaned in closer and took a deep breath. She smelled heavenly. I closed my eyes and tried to push these thoughts out of my head. We danced in silence. As the song ended, Liza pulled away. She looked into my eyes. I wasn't sure what to do. My heart was telling me to kiss her, but my head was telling me to walk away. Blake Shelton's "Who are you when I'm not looking" began playing. Liza's eyes lingered on my lips. I slowly leaned in. As we grew closer, she licked her lips in anticipation.

"Walker," she whispered.

Just as we were about to make contact, I heard someone yell out my name. I pulled back instantly and looked around.

"Walker fucking Moore!"

Mitchell Cunningham walked over as I let go of Liza and took a few steps back. I smiled and shook Mitchell's hand.

"I can't believe I'm running into you here in the middle of Hicksville, Walker." I laughed as I looked back at Liza.

Liza was eyeing Mitchell, and I didn't like the way she was looking at him. Mitchell turned to see who I was looking at, perking up the second he saw Liza.

"Well, who do we have here?" Mitchell asked.

Liza smiled, waiting for me to introduce her.

"Mitchell, this is Liza Morris," I said. "She's an old friend. We grew up together."

Mitchell took her hand and kissed it.

I leaned in and said, "Take a look at the left hand."

Liza shot me a dirty look. I shrugged and winked.

"Oh, damn. You're engaged," Mitchell said. "That sucks, sweetheart." He turned back to me. "Shit, dude. I thought you and Jessica were together. Jessica said y'all were getting married soon."

Liza and I both blurted, "What?"

Mitchell looked between Liza and me.

"You're getting married?" Liza asked.

"No. I mean…uh…" I stuttered. "When did you talk to Jessica, Mitchell?"

Mitchell still looked confused as hell. "Um…I saw her earlier today."

"Where?" I asked.

"Country club. Both our parents are members," he said, still eyeing both Liza and me. "Do you want to tell me why Jess is saying y'all are getting married when you're engaged to another girl?"

Liza laughed. "*We're* not engaged. I'm engaged to someone else."

I tilted my head and looked at her. "I thought you hadn't said yes yet?"

Liza's smile faded. "Well, when were you going to tell everyone about your engagement?"

"When I actually get engaged. I haven't asked Jessica to marry me yet."

Mitchell started laughing. "What a damn clusterfuck this is. Y'all all need to get your shit together."

"What does that mean?"

Mitchell took a few steps closer. "Dude. What I walked up on was not just two old friends just having a dance."

I shoved him a little. "Bullshit. You didn't walk up on anything."

He shook his head. "If you say so."

"Yeah, I say so."

Mitchell held his hands up and took a few steps back. "It was a pleasure to meet you, Liza," he said.

Liza nodded and Mitchell walked away. When I turned back to her, I swear she had tears in her eyes.

"I'm ready to go home. I'm not feeling so well."

I nodded and took her hand, but she instantly pulled away from me.

"I'll um…I'll look for Ava. You look for Jase. I'll meet y'all at the truck." I said.

Liza nodded, walking into the crowd of people dancing. I looked around for Ava, but I couldn't find her. I saw Liza walk out the front door, so I pulled out my phone and sent Ava and Jase a text telling them that we were leaving because Liza was sick. Then I followed Liza.

I rounded the corner and watched as she paused next to someone's truck, leaned over, and threw up.

"Fuck," I said, running my hand through my hair. I ran over and pulled Liza's hair back as she threw up again and again. "Damn it, Liza. How the hell much did you drink?"

She started crying as she looked up at me. "I don't know."

Jase and Ava appeared, running toward us.

"What's wrong with her?" Jase asked as he placed his hand on Liza's back.

"I just had too much to drink, Jase. That's all. I don't normally drink like that and then…" She stopped talking and shook her head.

"Then what, honey?" Ava said. "What upset you?"

Liza briefly met my gaze, but looked away. I stepped back and blinked slowly, thinking back to just a bit ago when she'd looked at me with pleading eyes. *Did Liza still have feelings for me, or was I imagining it?*

No, she was drunk—her actions probably had no meaning.

Ava rubbed her hand up and down Liza's back. "Liza, honey, are you okay? Can you make it to Walker's truck?"

Liza stood up and Ava handed her a tissue to wipe her mouth. She slowly nodded and said, "Yeah, I feel better, actually, now that I've thrown up."

Jase put his arm around Liza's waist and led her through the parking lot. "Yeah," he said, "you probably got some of that alcohol out of your system. Come on, let's get home and sneak you up to your room like we use to when we were in high school."

Liza chuckled and rested her head on Jase's shoulder. A tinge of jealousy raced through my blood—Liza was leaning on Jase instead of me.

I pulled up and parked behind Layton's truck. It was after midnight, and Jase and Ava had both passed out in the back seat. I tried to wake them, but had no luck. I got out and opened the passenger-side door. Liza had fallen asleep almost immediately after getting into the truck. I unbuckled her seatbelt and took her in my arms before carrying her to the back door. She was light as a feather. I had to admit that I loved having her in my arms.

I was relieved to find the back door open. I attempted to close it behind me without making a lot of noise. I made my way through the kitchen and living room and started up the stairs. I pushed open Liza's bedroom door and gently laid her on the bed. I turned on the desk lamp and when it lit up her room and I couldn't help but smile. It had been years since I'd been in Liza's room. I glanced at all the pictures on her photo board. Most of them were of Liza and me; some were with Jase and Ava.

Liza groaned, and I walked over to her. I helped her take off her boots placing each one quietly on the floor, then pulled the blankets out from under her and tucked her in. I sat on the bed and pushed her hair out of her face.

Liza opened her eyes and said, "Walker, I missed you."

I gave Liza a grin and said, "I missed you, too, Liza."

Her eyes moved across my face, like she was searching for an answer. She took a shaky breath and said, "It scares me."

I cocked my head. "What scares you?"

Liza sucked in her lower lip. "How much I want you to kiss me."

I swallowed hard as I stood up. Then I leaned over and kissed her on the forehead. "Goodnight, Liza," I whispered.

She closed her eyes and said, "Night, Walker."

For a few minutes, I just watched her sleep. When I heard the door creak open, I turned to see Jase there.

"Is she okay?" he asked.

I nodded and turned to leave, but Jase grabbed me by the arm and stopped me. He gave me an intense look.

"I see the way you look at her, Walker. And I see the way she looks at you. You're both in committed relationships, so please don't do something stupid."

I glanced back over to Liza. "I love Jessica. I would never do anything to hurt her. But I can't stop my feelings for Liza, Jase. She's like a sister to me."

The corner of his mouth pulled up into a slight smile. "Uh-huh. Like a *sister*. I'll see ya in a few hours."

I gave him a quick nod and walked out of Liza's room. The whole way out to my truck, I tried to make sense out of the feelings running rampant in my head. Ava had woken up and moved to the front seat where she was leaning against the passenger window. When I started the truck she groaned.

"Oh God, I'm never drinking again."

I laughed and put the truck in reverse and started to head down the driveway. I looked over to the house and gasped when I saw Liza standing at her window with her bedroom light on, watching me drive off.

I wiped the sweat from my forehead and leaned against my truck. "Shit, it's hot out."

Layton laughed. "Welcome home! Just think, it's not even summer yet."

I rolled my eyes and took a swig from my water. The cattle had been hanging around us the last hour. Hoping for an early feeding.

I looked over to see my father finishing up with the fence repair. Jase placed some tools in the back of the ranch truck and sighed. "I'm never drinking again. Ever."

Layton laughed and slapped Jase on the back. "What's the matter, son? Can't handle your alcohol?"

My dad chuckled. He was just about finished with the fence repair.

Jase grabbed a bottle of water from the cooler and shook his head. "I guess not, because I feel like shit."

"How was Liza feeling?" I asked.

Jase shrugged. "I guess she's okay. She woke up all happy, then grabbed her damn Kindle and curled up on the sofa in the den." Jase looked over to Layton. "Dad, I still think it's unfair that she gets to do nothing and I have to work my ass off."

Layton raised his eyebrows at Jase. "Do you want to run this ranch someday, son?"

Jase smiled. "Hell, yeah, I do, Dad."

Layton shrugged. "There you go. Liza doesn't. Stop being a pansy-ass and man up."

I threw my head back and laughed. Jase gave me the finger and shook his head.

Jase let out a breath and said, "This is going to be a long summer. I can see it now."

I pushed off the truck and shoved Jase, making him spill his water down his chest.

"Nah, it's going to be one hell of a summer!"

Jase dropped the water and took off running after me. We spent the next ten minutes running around like two ten year olds again. My father finally told us to knock it off and get in the truck. We both jumped into the bed and just sat silently all the way back to the main barn. I closed my eyes and took in all the smells. I loved being home. I hoped like hell Jessica would love it as much as I did. I opened my eyes and pulled out my phone. I had a text, so I opened it up.

**Jessica**: *Oh my gosh. I'm having a blast. Getting massages now, then we're getting our hair done at some salon my mother insisted we go to. Then we're checking out a new restaurant. Miss you and love you!*

I sighed. I had feeling that, once Jessica got here, she'd be far from happy.

# Five

## Liza

I walked out of the barn and ran smack into Walker.

"Shit," we both said.

I had to keep myself from moaning as I looked at him. He was covered in sweat and not wearing a shirt. Lord, why did his body have to look so good?

"Oh…um…hey there, Walker. Whatcha up to?" I asked, trying to avoid looking at him. He glanced at my left hand before meeting my gaze. He seemed to be doing this every time we saw each other. I wasn't sure whether he was looking for the ring he gave me, or checking for my engagement ring.

"Just got done unloading some feed. I need to saddle up a horse and check the fence line. You feel like going for a ride?"

*Jesus, I wish he would put his shirt back on.* The tattoo on his arm was amazing. The design was intricate and the colors beautiful. I could stare at it for hours. I looked him in the eyes and focused on his baby blue eye. "Sure," I said. "I'd love to."

"Can you saddle up Sweet Kate and Runner?"

"You want to ride Sweet Kate and Runner?" I asked as I glanced over to both stalls. They were the offspring of my father's prized racehorse, Lay it Low.

Walker gave me a smirk. "You afraid to ride Runner, Liza?"

"Pssh, no," I said, rolling my eyes. "I can ride any horse in this barn with no problem at all."

I glanced at Walkers massive chest and perfect abs. *Oh God. He has a V.*

I swallowed and said, "Are you on steroids or something?"

The moment it came out of my mouth, I regretted it.

Walker laughed and flexed his muscles. "Nope. This is called hard work, baby. It's all hard work. I know how to pump and how to pump it good."

My stomach did a crazy flip and I felt myself blushing. The image of Walker making love to me flooded my mind. I took a step back to break my trance.

"I'll, um, saddle up the horses." I turned and headed to the tack room.

"Good, I'll take a quick shower."

I spun around. "What? Where? Here? In the barn office?"

Walker stopped walking and looked at me. "Yeah, do you have a problem with that? Jase and I keep extra clothes in there."

My jaw dropped. This was not good. I shrugged and tried to laugh, as if I didn't care what Walker did. "I don't care where you take a shower,"

He walked to the end of the barn where the ranch hands' office was. It was more like a small apartment. Walker was formally staying in the fore-man's cabin on the ranch, but I heard Daddy telling Reed that Walker tended to sleep in the barn apartment so that he could get an early start with things on the ranch.

I smiled as I began getting the horses ready. Daddy had been talking about Walker to Reed last night. They were impressed with how hard Walker was working. They were planning on taking my mother and Court-ney on a cruise and letting Walker and Jase handle the ranch. I knew it would make Walker really happy to know our fathers trusted him enough to run things while they were gone.

When I got both horses saddled up and ready to go, I sat down on a hay bale and waited. "What is taking him so long?" I whispered to myself. I stood and walked toward the office door. I reached for the knob and paused for a second before I pushed it open. I stopped when I heard Walker on the phone.

"I'm glad you're having fun, Jessica. Nah, not much is going on here. Just working."

I pulled the door back, but left it cracked open as I stepped off to the side. I couldn't believe I was eavesdropping on Walker's phone call. But I was.

"I miss you, too. Damn, Jessica. Baby, I wish I could, but I can't."

*He paused, and I wondered what she wanted him to do.*

"I want to see you touch yourself, too, baby."

*Oh gag me.* I turned to leave but then I heard my name. "Liza is right outside the door. No, not much, we see each other every once in a while."

I leaned in closer.

"Jessica, we've talked about this. Liza and I are friends. The ring doesn't mean anything anymore."

I felt tears building in my eyes. I felt for the ring on my chest. I'd been wearing it, but tucking it into my shirt.

"Jess, for Christ's sake she's engaged. Yes. No, I haven't gone ring shopping yet."

I placed my hand on my stomach and was about to walk away when I decided I wasn't going to stand out here and wait for his ass. I turned and grabbed the doorknob, knocking as I opened the door. Walker spun around and looked at me. I went to say something but his hair was wet...and messy...he had on fresh clothes and—to make things worse—he was just putting on his stupid cowboy hat. My heart was beating and want pulled at my core. I quickly turned and walked away.

"Jessica, I have to go. I love you, baby. I'll talk to you later."

*Ugh. Double gag me. Asshole.*

I walked past the horses and made my way outside. Inhaling a deep breath of fresh air, I closed my eyes. The wind in the trees instantly calmed me.

"Liza? Are you okay?" Walker asked, placing his hand on my arm. I wanted to ignore the feeling that zipped through my body when he touched me.

*Keith. I love Keith.*

I put a fake smile on my face. "Yeah. I just didn't know you were on the phone. I'm sorry I just walked in like that. I was wondering what was taking so long."

Walker gave me a weak smile. He nodded toward the horses. "You ready to ride?"

I nodded and walked back over to the horses. After walking the horses out of the barn, we got on and rode in silence. I wanted to ask Walker why Jessica was worried about me, but I knew it was probably the same reason Keith was worried about Walker. I peeked over at him—he was staring intently at the fence as we rode along.

I closed my eyes and just let Sweet Kate follow Runner and Walker. The sounds of my home comforted me more than I'd realized. The closer we got the river, the better I felt. I loved sitting down by the river and just doing nothing. My mother and I used to go and put out a blanket and sit for hours, reading. I'd inherited my love of reading from my mother and Walker's mom, Courtney.

I smiled as I thought of all the times we'd sat and just talked for hours, just Mom and me. Walker's voice pulled me out of my thoughts.

"Thinking?"

"What?"

He laughed. "Are you thinking? You had your eyes closed—that's what you used to do when you were thinking. You'd just tune everyone else out and...think."

I giggled and nodded. "Yeah, I was remembering all the times I came down here with my mother. I didn't realize how much I'd missed home. I'm going to miss it if..."

I stopped talking and Walker looked away. "You could really leave all this behind, Liza? Your family, friends...all of it?"

I caught myself gnawing on my lip. "Should we stop and let the horses get a drink?"

Walker chuckled and shook his head. "Sure."

I walked along the riverbank as we let Sweet Kate and Runner graze for a bit. I heard a noise and turned around to see Walker running toward me wearing nothing but his boxers. I started taking quick steps backwards before I turned and went into a full run.

"Stay away from me, Walker Moore! I swear to God, if—"

Walker picked up and threw me over his shoulder.

"Walker! Put me down *now*!" I yelled.

Walker laughed and said, "I don't think so, darlin'. We're taking a dip."

I was about to yell when Walker jumped off the riverbank. The water in this part of the river was deep and, with all the spring rain, it was probably even deeper than normal. I screamed as the cold water hit me. Walker laughed as we came up from under the water. He let go, and I stood up in waist-deep water.

"You asshole! I'm soaking wet now."

Walker threw his head back and laughed. "Hey, you said you were hot! I did you a favor."

I tried to push him under as he grabbed my arms and pushed me back. He slipped and fell as I landed on him. I wrapped my legs around him and hit him over and over again as we both laughed. Walker stood up and that's when it hit me—I had my legs wrapped around him tight, and I could feel his dick pressing into me. I was instantly turned on, and wanted nothing more than to push myself into him to relieve the pressure.

Walker stopped laughing and his smile slowly faded away. His eyes moved down my face and landed on my lips. I slowly ran my tongue along my bottom lip before I bit down on it. When my eyes landed on his lips, I knew what I was wanting was wrong.

I slowly unwrapped my legs from around him as he set me down. He pushed my hair back, away from my eyes. He placed his hand on the side of my face and smiled.

"You're breathtaking, Liza."

I swallowed hard. I wanted to throw myself into his arms and beg him to take me right here in the river. Keith would never have done anything like this. He was so serious.

*Keith.*

I took a few steps back and said, "We'd better get going."

Walker cleared his throat and grinned. "Yeah, probably." He turned and began walking out of the river. "I just need to dry off a bit or I'll never get my jeans on."

I nodded, even though I knew he couldn't see me. "Okay," I whispered. I leaned against Sweet Kate as I tried to catch my breath.

I stood at the kitchen sink and looked out to see Layton talking to Walker. I hadn't seen Walker in four days, not since our ride…and our little dip in the river. I wasn't sure what my father and Walker were talking about, but it appeared to be serious.

"Hey mom?"

"Mmm?" My mother had her nose in her Kindle.

"Do you know what Daddy is talking to Walker about?"

She grunted and I shook my head, then hit her with the towel I was holding. "Mom!"

"Hey!" she said, setting down her Kindle. "I was at a good part, Taylor Elizabeth!"

I rolled my eyes. "Ugh, don't call me that, mom."

She pushed her chair back. "It really warms my heart that you despise your name."

I giggled as I turned back and picked up another plate to dry. "So, do you know what they're talking about?"

My mother peeked out the window and smiled. "Probably the Kentucky trip."

My phone beeped. I picked it up and smiled when I saw I had a text from Keith.

**Keith**: *Got service for a bit. How are you baby?*
**Me**: *I'm good. How is the hiking going?*
**Keith**: *All I can think about is fucking you.*

My jaw dropped. Keith had never talked to me like that before. I glanced over at my mother and quickly walked outside.

**Me**: *Um…*
**Keith**: *I was thinking about you and had to go off and take care of myself as I looked at your picture, baby. I imagined I was fucking you against a tree. I hate being away from you.*

I was instantly wet as I closed my eyes and pictured Keith doing just that. I opened my eyes and texted him back.

**Me**: *Where are you now?*
**Keith**: *Standing on top of a mountain not moving because I have a signal.*
**Me**: *LOL! I miss you.*
**Keith**: *I miss you, too. I'd better go. Love you, Liza.*

I didn't hear Walker approaching, but I heard him laugh. I lifted my head quickly to see him, still with my father. Daddy turned and headed over to me; Walker followed.

"Liza, you feel like going on a road trip?" Daddy asked.

Looking down, I quickly typed a goodbye to Keith.

**Me**: *Miss u. Love u.*

I stood up and smiled. "Road trip? Where?"

Walker was looking down at the ground, kicking a rock around with his boot.

"Kentucky. It was just gonna be me and Walker, but I'd love to spend some father-daughter time with you."

My heart just about burst with joy. "Yes! Daddy, I'd love to do that."

Walker jerked his head up. I wasn't sure whether or not he was displeased that my father had invited me along.

"All right, then. Go pack up, baby girl. We leave in the morning. Early."

I clapped and skipped a little.

Walker cracked a smile and shook his head. I headed into the house and rushed past my mother.

"Where in the world are you going in such a rush?" she asked.

I called over my shoulder, "I'm going to Kentucky with Daddy!"

She laughed as I took the stairs two at a time. I pulled my suitcase from under the bed. I couldn't believe I'd have a whole week with my father! *And* with Walker!

*Wait. What? Damn it.* I sat down on my bed, my head in my hands.

I'd just been daydreaming of my boyfriend fucking me, and now I was excited about spending time with Walker. I moaned in frustration as I fell back on the bed. There was a faint knock at the door. I sat up to see my mother standing there. The smile on her face told me we were about to have a talk. I motioned for her to come in. "What's up, Mom?"

She scrunched up her nose in that oh-so-cute way of hers and shrugged. "Just thought maybe we could have a heart-to-heart."

"Sure. About what?"

She sat down on my left side and reached for my hand. "Where's your ring?"

I looked down at my finger. "Oh, I took it off yesterday after Courtney asked if I wanted to help her plant some things in the garden."

My mother nodded. She pulled my necklace out from under my shirt until she held the double heart ring. "Walker gave this to you before y'all left for school, didn't he?"

"Yeah, he did."

"You wear it around your neck every day, Liza."

I narrowed one eye at my mother. "So?"

She dropped the ring and sighed. "I remember the first time I saw your father."

The smile on her face made me smile. I pulled my knees up and got ready for a story. I loved when my mother talked about her and my father. Their love was so amazing.

"Was it love at first sight?" I asked as I wiggled my eyebrows.

She made a face and said, "Yes and no. I was attracted to him beyond belief. But he also annoyed the hell out of me."

I giggled. "Daddy? Never!"

She nodded, walked over to my dresser, and leaned against it. "Oh, yes. Believe it. He was charming, but arrogant. All I really wanted to do was smack him upside his head. But something else started happening. When he was near me, it was as if all the air was being sucked out of the room. When he smiled at me..." She shook her head and laughed. "God, when he smiled at me, it felt as if all my troubles were gone." She placed her fingers up to her lips. "His kiss...his kiss is like magic. It completely takes my breath away, yet fills my entire body with life. If that makes sense."

I nodded quickly. My smile faded as I looked out the window and then back to my mother.

"Mom, how do you know if it's...real?"

"What do you mean, Liza?"

I sucked in a deep breath. "How do you know if the love you feel for someone is real?" I felt tears building as I looked back out the window. "Keith wants to take me away from here. He wants me to give up everything I love and move to Dallas to make a life with him. I'm not sure I can do that."

I swallowed as I felt my mother sit next to me and take my hand. "Liza, look at me."

I met her gaze.

"How does Keith make you feel when he smiles at you? Or when he kisses you? When he tells you how beautiful you are?"

I thought back to the other day in the river with Walker. When he placed his hand on the side of my face and told me I was breathtaking, it had made my heart race. My stomach had felt like a million butterflies were dancing inside.

I felt a tear roll down my face. I knew why I was holding back with Keith. I didn't feel the butterflies when he told me how pretty I was. His kiss didn't fill my body with life, even though I did feel something.

My mother wiped my tear away. "Liza, if Keith makes you feel like your father makes me feel, then leaving to be with him should be the easiest decision of your life."

I sucked in a breath.

She smiled and stood up. "Finish packing, sweetheart. Then let's go for a walk." I nodded as I looked down. My mother was about to round the corner when she stopped. I looked up when she said, "You might want to also ask yourself something else."

I smiled and asked, "What's that?"

"How do you feel when Walker smiles at you?"

My smile faded as she walked away and headed downstairs.

# Six

## Walker

I sat in the back seat of Layton's truck and stared at the laptop. I was trying to figure out the program Layton used to keep track of the horses information. Liza was sleeping up in the front, and her little noises were driving me insane. I couldn't think. I closed the laptop and pulled out my phone.

I had a text from Jessica. I smiled as I opened it. I hadn't even heard my phone go off.

> **Jessica**: *Seven tonight your time. I can sneak away. Can you Facetime me?*

I stared at the text message. I started to type a response.

> **Me**: *I don't think I can.*
> **Jessica**: *Hey baby! You don't think you can what?*
> **Me**: *Facetime you. I'm driving up to Kentucky with Layton.*
> **Jessica**: *What?*
> **Me**: *Your last text to me. You asked me to Facetime you.*
> **Jessica**: *Oh. Damn. I thought maybe we could play around.*

**Me**: *Believe me, I'd love to let off some steam.*
**Jessica**: *I'd like to see you let it off. Text me when you get to KY and check into your hotel. Maybe we can work out a phone call. I want to hear you when you come.*

"We're here," Layton said. He reached across the center console and shook Liza.

**Me**: *We're pulling up now. Are you free?*
**Jessica**: *No. :( Sorry, baby. Later maybe. Gotta run. Love you!*

I sighed as I adjusted my aching, hard dick. I smiled when I saw the hotel. "Mountain High Lodge and Resort" I read aloud.

"Oh, Daddy. It's beautiful here." Liza said.

Layton chuckled. "Yeah, this place is in the middle of nowhere, but it's the closet place I could get us to the horse ranch. Come on, let's go get checked in. There's no rest for the weary. Y'all need to take showers and head out."

"What?" Liza and I said at the same time.

Layton got out of the truck and made his way around to the passenger side. He opened Liza's door as he talked to the doorman.

I got out of the truck and stretched. It felt like I'd been in that truck for a week.

Layton turned to me and said, "They'll get the luggage. Let's go check in."

Fifteen minutes later, I was in a room overlooking the Kentucky Appalachians. "Wow," I whispered. My phone rang and I took it out of my pocket. It was Layton.

"Miss me already?" I asked.

"Haha. Take a shower and pack an overnight bag."

I checked the time. It was two in the afternoon and I was ready to relax for the rest of the day. "Can I ask why?"

"You and Liza are heading out to the ranch this afternoon and staying the night. I want you to check out the horses before I get there. I want Liza there, too. She has a good eye for horses. I'll come out first thing in the morning and see how you did."

My jaw dropped to the ground. "You want *me* to go to the ranch first?"

"I do believe that's what I said. Do you have a problem with that, Walker? You assured me you were ready to take on this side of the business."

I swallowed. "Yes, sir. I mean, I won't lie. I'm pretty sure I just shit my pants."

Layton laughed. "Make me proud, son. Now get showered up. It's a long drive out to the ranch."

"Yes, sir. I'll be fast."

I quickly stripped out of my clothes, pumped my fist and jumped into the shower. I was going to make both my father and Layton proud. I was going to show them both that I'd been paying attention all those years.

Liza stared out the window of the rented truck. Layton had arranged it all ahead of time. I let out a breath as I watched the road.

"Can you please stop doing that?" Liza asked.

I gave her a quick glance. "Stop doing what?"

"Sighing. It's annoying."

I rolled my eyes. "Well excuse me, princess, if I'm a little nervous. It's not every day that the man you've looked up to your whole life gives you the opportunity to prove that you really do know your shit."

I could feel her eyes on me when she asked, "You really do love my dad, don't you?"

I was dumbfounded. "Of course I do, Liza. He's like a second father to me."

"Fine, you're nervous. Keep the sighing to yourself."

"What the hell is wrong with you?" I asked.

She shook her head. "I don't want to be here. I thought I was going to be spending time with my father. Instead, I'm driving out to some remote-ass horse ranch with you."

It felt like a knife in my chest. "I'm not really sure what the hell I did to you, but I'm sorry I'm making your trip miserable."

I laughed, "Uh, yeah, you did."

"No, I didn't."

"Yes. You. Did."

She turned and looked at me. "No. I. Didn't. Asshole."

I felt heat move through my body. "What's wrong, Jessica? Missing out on phone sex with your precious fiancé, Keith?"

She had tears in her eyes. "My name is, Liza. Not Jessica, you fucker. And I believe it's you and *Jessica* who like to get nasty over the phone." She turned her whole body toward the window.

My whole body slumped in the seat. I couldn't believe what a dick I'd just been. "Liza, I'm sorry. I didn't mean to call you Jessica. I didn't mean any of it."

She threw up her hand, brushing me off. "It doesn't matter. Please don't talk to me."

We rode for another hour and a half in silence. I was almost positive that I was on the wrong road. Liza was asleep with her headphones on. I pulled up the GPS on my phone.

*Nothing.*

I checked the gas gauge and saw that I only had twenty-six miles left on this tank. I hadn't seen a gas station in miles. I nudged Liza and she startled, pulling off her headphones.

"What? Are we there?" she asked.

"I think I missed an exit."

"What? How did you miss the exit?"

I shook my head. "I don't know, Liza. I just missed it. We are in the middle of nowhere, I have no signal, and we're about out of gas."

"What?" She picked up her phone. "Oh my God. My GPS is disconnected!"

I rolled my eyes. "Like I said, Liza, there's no cell coverage."

"So you just kept driving? Like an idiot?"

I slammed on the brakes and pulled to the side of the road.

"What are you doing?"

I opened the door, jumped out, and walked around the front of the truck. I pulled the passenger door open and handed the keys to Liza. "You drive."

She laughed, but her smiled quickly faded. "Are you serious?"

"Yeah. You drive."

She folded her arms over her chest. "I don't want to drive."

I shrugged. "Neither do I."

"Well, someone's going to have to do it," Liza said. She unbuckled and pushed me out of the way as she jumped out of the truck.

I turned and walked to the back of the truck. I pulled the tailgate down and jumped up to sit there. I could hear Liza mumbling something. I watched her as she tried to find a cell signal. After ten minutes of walking around with her phone in the air, Liza leaned against the passenger side door. I lay back in the truck bed.

"I'm not driving!" She yelled.

"Neither am I!" I yelled back.

I sat up when I heard a car horn. I looked at my watch. We'd been sitting on the side of the road for over an hour. Neither one of us had budged when it came to driving. Liza was sitting inside the truck when an older lady got out of her truck and approached us.

Liza got out of the truck and said, "Thank goodness you came by."

The older lady looked at Liza and then me. "Are y'all broken down?"

I shook my head. I was a little dizzy from the sun. "No, ma'am. Just lost."

She laughed. "I see. Well, where are you trying to get to?"

"McMurphy Ranch." Liza and I said at the same time. We both slowly turned and looked at each other.

"McMurphy Ranch? You're about an hour from there."

"What?" I blurted.

"No," Liza said. "Please don't say that. We've been driving for hours. I mean, we just drove up from Texas, and my father made us head straight for the ranch. I fell asleep and we lost the GPS signal and this idiot just kept driving. Probably dreaming about Jessica."

"Hey, you're the one who's always lost in thought. At least I'm not walking around pretending to be—"

"Stop. Both of you." The older lady had her fingers on her temples. "My God. I haven't heard this kind of arguing since my Harold died five years ago."

"Oh, I'm so sorry," Liza said.

I took a deep breath. "I'm sorry. We're tired and hungry."

"I have cabins that I rent. I'm afraid they're all full, but I do have a room that you're more than welcome to stay in for the night. I'll get you on the right road in the morning."

I closed my eyes and turned around. *Great. Just fucking great.*

"Oh, that would be wonderful. Thank you so very much. Walker, isn't that nice of…"

The older woman smiled. "Mrs. Jenkins."

"Isn't that nice of Mrs. Jenkins, Walker? To let us stay at her place?"

I glared at Liza. "No, Liza, it isn't wonderful. I'm supposed to be at the McMurphy Ranch, looking at horses. I'm not supposed to be here." I kicked a rock and yelled out. "I'm not supposed to be here! Motherfucker!"

Mrs. Jenkins gave me a polite smile. "I have a phone at my place. You're more than welcome to use it. If you'd like to head to the ranch, I can show you the way, but you'll be getting there after sundown. You can't really look at horses in the dark."

Liza stepped in between Mrs. Jenkins and me. "How far is your place? We're very low on gas."

She smiled at Liza. "I'm about three miles down the road. I have gas, so we can get you topped off enough to get you to the gas station. Now let's get you off the side of the road. Can you follow me?"

Liza glared at me. "If you don't mind, may I ride with you Mrs. Jenkins?"

I grabbed Liza's arm. "Your dad would be pissed if I let you go off with a stranger."

Her eyes searched my entire face before she looked me in the eye. "I've been with one for the last hour."

I dropped her arm and she walked over to Mrs. Jenkins' trucks and got in. I got in the truck, started it, and pulled out behind Mrs. Jenkins. I followed her almost exactly two miles to a long, paved driveway. The driveway itself must have been three miles long. As we drove, we passed dirt roads that branched off. Those must have led to the cabins Mrs. Jenkins had mentioned. Finally, we pulled up to a large house. There were two couples sitting on the front porch—one sitting on a swing and the other in rocking chairs. I put the truck in park and grabbed my bag and Liza's from the backseat. As I made my way to the porch, Mrs. Jenkins was already introducing Liza to the two couples.

"We're here for our honeymoon," The lady on the swing said as she looked at the guy sitting next to her.

"Ten year anniversary for us," The guy in the rocking chair said.

Liza smiled and reached her hand out. Mrs. Jenkins introduced me and after a few minutes of small talk we followed her into the house.

"I turned the house into a bed and breakfast after my husband died." Mrs. Jenkins said as we entered the house. She walked around a counter and pulled down a key, which she handed to us. "Breakfast will be served at seven sharp. You have your own private bathroom, so you can clean up and get some sleep."

I looked down at the key. "Do you have two rooms? I mean, we'll pay of course."

She frowned. "No, I only have the one. But there is a queen bed in there." She winked and turned as she headed to the stairs. "Now follow me. I'll show you to your room."

As I followed Mrs. Jenkins and Liza—who looked like she was about to be sick—up the stairs, I couldn't decide who was going to be more pissed about Liza and me sharing a room: Layton or Jessica.

# Seven

## Liza

**M**rs. Jenkins shut the door as she smiled at Walker and me. We stood there staring at the door for way too long before we finally accepted our fate.

Walker seemed to be evaluating the room, same as me. There was no sofa, no other chairs. Nothing but a bed.

"I'll just sleep on the floor." He dropped the bags and walked through the bathroom door. "Do you mind if I take a shower first?"

I shook my head "no" as I sat down on the bed. I was tired. Hungry. Angry. Upset. And, most of all, confused. A part of me was happy that Walker and I were stuck here alone together. The other part was feeling guilty about this happiness.

I pulled out my phone and found that we still had no signal, so I used the landline to call my father's cell. When he picked up, I took a deep breath.

"Daddy, it's me, Liza."

"Liza! Where the hell are y'all? I've been calling both of your phones and getting nothing."

"I'm so sorry, Daddy. I must have put the wrong address in the GPS. We got so lost. We're about an hour from the ranch. Walker is just torn up inside, Daddy, and it's all my fault."

"It's okay, sweetheart. As long as you're both okay. Where are you?"

"We're at a little bed and breakfast out in the middle of nowhere. The owner, Mrs. Jenkins, was nice enough to put us up for the night. She's going to get us back on the right path tomorrow. Do you think you could give Walker a few hours tomorrow morning? You know, to look over the horses before you get there?"

"Yes, of course. I know how much this trip meant to him. Just make sure you eat and get some sleep darlin'. I love you."

I smiled. "I will, Daddy. I'm sorry I messed this up for Walker."

My father chuckled. "It's okay honey. I know he's going to do great tomorrow. Sleep well. I'll see you tomorrow. Late morning or early afternoon."

I smiled. "Thank you, Daddy. Night. Love you."

"Love you, too."

I hung up the phone and let out a sigh.

"Why did you do that?"

I jumped and spun around to see Walker ...in a towel. In *only* a towel. *Oh for the love of God.*

I looked away and said, "Why did I do what?"

I heard Walker rummaging through his bag as he walked back to the bathroom. "Tell your father it was your fault. It was *my* fault."

I slowly turned around and looked him in the eye. "Because I know how much this means to you. And, well, I want you to succeed. I mean, I know you will, because you're, well, I mean... you're good at everything. You um, everything you touch...or...uh..." I shook my head and turned away. "Walker, can you please get dressed?"

"Oh, yeah. Sorry." The bathroom door shut and I let out a breath. I kicked off my sneakers. I couldn't wait to strip out of my clothes and get into something comfortable.

When I heard the bathroom door open again, I was scared to death to see what in the world Walker might be wearing. When Walker put his hands on my shoulders, I held my breath. It was like I'd been hit by lighting. He turned me around and looked into my eyes. I took in his body from top to bottom. He had put on a pair of cotton pants that barely hung onto his hips. The tight tank top he wore made his chest seem even bigger. I wanted to grab his muscular arms and just feel them. When Walker took hold of my shirt, I sucked in a breath. He gently lifted it, pulling it over my head. His eyes grew big as they landed on my chest. I was wearing a tan lace bra that I'd just bought a few days ago. I was internally fist pumping, thankful that I'd put this on rather than a sports bra.

Walker moved his hand to my breast. My breathing picked up as my chest heaved. When his finger touched my skin, I gasped. He moved his finger along the edge of my bra as he watched my chest rise and fall with each breath. I was beginning to feel weak in the knees, so I grabbed onto his arms. He quickly met my gaze. I'd never in my life felt the feelings that were pulsing through my body. I was desperate for him. Desperate for his kiss, his touch—anything he was willing to give me.

Walker slid his hands down and unbuttoned my jean shorts. I swallowed hard as he squatted down to push them from my hips and down my legs. I held onto his shoulders as I stepped out of the shorts. Walker looked up at me and the ache in my abdomen grew stronger. He slowly ran his hand up my leg as he stood up. Everywhere he touched left a burning trail. I closed my eyes, praying that this moment wouldn't end any time soon.

Walker stood before me, his eyes searching my face intently. He seemed to be seeking permission to take the next step. His fingertips lightly touched my arms as he moved his hands up to cup my face in his hands. He leaned down and our lips were about to touch when someone knocked on the door. We jumped back, away from each other.

"Liza? Walker? I heated up some food for you if you'd like to come down and eat."

The lump in my throat kept me silent. We stared at each for what seemed like forever.

Walker seemed to snap out of the trance first. "I'm sorry..." he whispered as he turned toward the door. "Thank you, Mrs. Jenkins. We'll be right down."

My eyes burned as I realized what had just happened. I covered my mouth with my hand before grabbing my bag and heading into the bathroom. I shut the door, turned the cold water on, and splashed my face.

I looked up at myself in the mirror. I couldn't believe we'd almost cheated. I'd been about to kiss him. We were about to...

The knock on the door pulled me back to reality.

"Liza, are you okay?" Walker asked.

My voice cracked. "Um, yeah. I'll be right out."

"If you want to take a quick shower, I'm sure it would be okay...I'll um...I'll just head on down there."

I wiped my tears away and cleared my throat. The only word I could manage was, "Okay."

When I heard the bedroom door close, I turned on the shower, took off the rest of my clothes, got in, and stood under the hot water. I cried harder than I ever had in my life.

As I walked down the stairs, I heard laughter. Walker and a woman. And that woman sure as hell wasn't Mrs. Jenkins. I stopped and peeked around the corner. My breath caught at the sight of Walker. He hadn't shaved in a few days and the stubble was even more of a turn-on then his beautiful, blue eyes. I bit my lip when I saw him smile at someone. Then I saw her.

A beautiful blonde smiled back at Walker. Heat instantly bubbled up as I forced my feet to take me into the kitchen. I cleared my throat and Walker and the blonde both turned toward me. I cocked my head at Walker. His smile faded just a bit as he looked down and took a bite of what looked like chicken and dumplings.

"You must be Liza. Walker was just telling me how y'all have known each other since you were babies."

I gave her a weak smile as I nodded. "Yeah. We've known each other a long time," I said. I wanted to roll my eyes at myself. What a stupid response.

The blonde giggled. "I'm Michelle, by the way. I help Mrs. Jenkins out sometimes."

*Oh gosh. One close encounter with Walker and I forget how to behave.* I smiled warmly. "I'm sorry, I'm not sure where my manners are right now. I think I'm just..." I looked at Walker, who was waiting for my response. "Tired. I'm really tired. It's been a very long day." I sat down, glancing at Walker, and thanked Michelle as she set a bowl of chicken and dumplings in front of me.

"Walker here was telling me a pretty lame joke to cheer me up," Michelle said, winking at Walker.

I tried to push away the jealousy. "Really?" I asked.

Michelle's smile faded. "My husband left this morning. He's in the Navy and he'll be gone for six months."

My mouth fell open. "Oh...that has to be really hard."

She smiled and nodded. "It is, but he will be heading home for good after this."

I couldn't help but smile back. "Well, thank him for his service. I'm glad this is the last time he'll leave you."

Michelle wiped her hands on her apron and leaned back against the counter. "Thank you. Walker said the same exact thing."

I peeked over at Walker and found him staring back. I looked back down at my bowl and focused on only eating.

We stared at the bed. Finally, Walker grabbed a pillow and a blanket that was sitting at the end of the bed. As he laid the blanket out on the floor, my heart hurt in ways it shouldn't. I wanted to tell him to sleep in the bed, that it would be okay. But with what happened earlier, I wasn't so sure. I watched as he tried to get comfortable.

"Night, Liza," he said.

I was about to say something when my cell phone rang. I was shocked that I had a signal. When I saw Keith's name I was overcome with guilt.

"Hello?" It was a bad connection, and I could barely hear him.

"Liza? Can you hear me? Baby? Can you hear me?"

I looked at Walker on the floor and closed my eyes. "Yep, I can hear you."

"Hey, baby! It's so good to hear your voice."

"You too," I said, trying to keep my voice down.

"Have you missed me?"

"Yes. You?" I opened my eyes and saw Walker looking at me.

Keith let out a small moan. "More than you know. I want to feel your warmth. I miss what it feels like to make love to you."

I couldn't respond—not with Walker looking at me. I closed my eyes and imagined Walker kissing me. I imagined his touch, his eyes looking into mine. The moment I felt the tear slip from my eyes, I stood up and turned my back to Walker.

"Keith, I can't really hear you. The connection is really bad."

"Are you at the hotel in Kentucky? I'll call you on the land line."

I shook my head. "No, um…I'm…well I'm at a…" the moment the phone went dead I said a silent prayer of thanks.

I put my phone on silent and set it back down on the end table. I took a deep breath and crawled into the bed, where I stared at the ceiling. I was so tired, but my body would not relax into sleep. I knew what I was about to do was wrong, but I was desperate. I needed sleep, and I knew the only way I would get it was is to be near him.

"Walker? Are you awake?" I whispered.

"Yes," he whispered back, his voice cracking.

We sat up at the same time. I took a shaky breath and said, "What happened earlier can't happen again."

Moonlight was shining in through the window, lighting up the room. Walker nodded. "I'm sorry. I don't know what came over me."

Swallowing hard, I spoke again. "I um…I can't sleep. When we were younger…"

"I would hold you until you fell asleep." I chewed on my lip as Walker whispered, "Liza…"

Tears streamed down my face. "Please—I'm so tired, Walker. I don't know what's happening. I'm so confused and I just want some sleep." I sobbed as our eyes met. "Please."

# Eight

## Walker

Listening to the only girl I've ever really loved ask me to hold her while she fell asleep was almost more than I could take. I closed my eyes and thought back to earlier, when we'd both finally let our guards down, almost doing the one thing I knew we both wanted. Promises we'd made to others were the only things holding us back. I'd cursed myself the whole way downstairs. I'd promised myself that I would never put Liza in that situation again, and here she was, asking me to hold her. All I really wanted to do was feel every inch of her body. Kiss her in places that I knew turned her on. I wondered if *Keith* knows those places.

"Please, Walker."

I stood up and grabbed the pillow, leaving the blanket on the floor. Once she fell asleep, I'd slip out of the bed and sleep on the floor. There was no way in hell I'd be able to sleep next to her all night.

Liza fell back onto her pillow and turned her back toward me as I crawled under the sheet. The moment I felt her body against me, I began a chant in my head: *You love Jessica. You only want Jessica.* I placed my arm around Liza and pulled her closer to me, but not close enough that she might feel my already hardening dick. *You love Jessica. You only want Jessica.*

I breathed in Liza's scent and was transported back to the day we'd said goodbye.

*Liza's parents were in Austin for a holiday benefit party. I'd snuck up into Liza's room, and we hadn't stopped kissing since shutting her bedroom door. Now we were on her bed and I had my dick pressed between her legs. She moaning quietly and I wanted to strip her down and make love to her once and for all, but something was stopping us. This last semester had been hard for both of us. Being away from Liza was starting to make me go crazy. I couldn't think straight anymore. I always wondered what she was doing. Where she was. Who she was with.*

*I moved my lips to her ear and kissed it. She wrapped her legs around me and pulled me closer.*

*"Oh, God. Walker...I'm going to come." She whispered as I pressed in harder. I bit her ear and she grabbed my arms, arching her back as she tried to hold back her moans of pleasure. I moved my lips to hers as I swallowed one moan after another. I loved that I could make her come like this. I couldn't help but wonder what it might feel like with me inside her. As Liza's orgasm began to wind down, she loosened her grip on me. I pulled away and smiled. Her chest was heaving and she was biting her lip.*

*"I miss you so much," I said, watching her chew on her lip. "I don't think I can keep doing this, Liza." I leaned down and kissed her, gently sucking on her lower lip. "I want to make love to you so bad, but I know the moment I do, I'm going to crave you even more. And you'll be gone." I watched as a tear slid down her face.*

*"What are you saying, Walker?" she asked. I knew from the look in her eyes that she was thinking the same thing that I was.*

*I moved off of her and sat on the edge of her bed. She adjusted her bra and shirt and sat next to me. She took a breath and asked, "Should we take a break from...us?"*

*I slowly nodded. "I can't focus, Liza."*

*"Neither can I. It's getting harder," she said, wiping her nose.*

*I took her hand and held it. Little did I know that would be the last time I'd kiss her.*

"Thank you," Liza whispered.

I held her next to me, keeping my dick away, but still keeping her close enough that she felt safe. Growing up, anytime she had a nightmare she'd text me and I'd sneak in through her bedroom window to hold her until she fell asleep. I'd sit there and watch her sleep for a while before heading home. I think one of those nights was when it finally hit me—I loved her and would do anything for her.

The sound of her steady breathing relaxed me. *Don't fall asleep.* I told myself. *Do. Not. Fall. Asleep.* My eyelids grew heavier as I closed them, telling myself I'd only sleep here for a few minutes.

*Beep. Beep. Beep.*

*What the fuck is that sound?*

*Beep. Beep. Beep.*

It must have been Liza's alarm. The moment she moved, my eyes sprung open. I was still holding her. I was still spooning Liza and my dick was pressed right against her. I was frozen. Too scared to move. Was she awake? She gently lifted my arm to move it off of her. *Shit.* I wondered if I should pretend to be asleep and spare us the embarrassment.

I kept my eyes closed as I listened to her move around the room. When I heard the bathroom door close, I rolled over and stared up at the ceiling. I sat up and swung my legs over and sat on the edge of the bed, but I couldn't help thinking about holding Liza all night. *All night.* The girl of my dreams had been in my arms all night. I shook my head and quickly reached for my jeans, then went to my bag to get a T-shirt. I was startled when my phone buzzed with Jessica's ring tone. I grabbed it from the desk and answered.

"Hello?"

"Hey, handsome. What are you doing?"

I ran my hand through my hair. *Oh you know. Sleeping with another woman in my arms.* "I'm in Kentucky, about to go look at some horses."

Jessica laughed. "Sounds like loads of fun."

"It's my life now."

She cleared her throat and asked, "Who are you with?"

I closed my eyes. "Layton and Liza."

"Liza's there? Why did she go?" Her voice was laced with hate.

Liza walked out of the bathroom, stopping to look at me. I watched as her eyes moved over my body. That's when I realized I hadn't put on my T-shirt yet.

"Hello? Are you going to answer me?"

"Um, to spend time with her dad, I guess."

Liza and I just stared at each other. This wasn't going to work. Us being together…alone.

Jessica made a funny sound and said, "Huh. Well, where are you right now? You sound distracted. Have you gone shopping for rings yet? When are you heading back to Texas?"

I turned away from Liza and whispered, "What the hell is this? Twenty questions?"

It sounded like she was crying. *Ah hell.*

"I'm going to be coming home early. Mother and I are tired of Europe. We're going to head back and spend some time in New York City. Would you like to meet us there?"

I dragged in a deep breath as I ran my free hand down my face. "I can't, Jessica. I'm sorry. You know I would if I could."

"Right. The ranch is more important."

I balled my fists up and tried to settle my slowly-building anger. "Why are you doing this? You know this is me. This is my life and if you don't want to be a part of…"

"Stop. I'm sorry." She began crying harder. "It's just that I miss you. I'm sorry I was being a bitch. I know this is your life now. I *do* want to be a part of it."

There was a knock at the door. "Jessica, I'm sorry but I really have to run."

"O-okay. I'm sorry."

I closed my eyes. "Me, too."

"I love you and miss you," she whispered.

Turning, I watched Liza pack up her stuff and throw her bag over her shoulder. As she walked by, I grabbed her arm. Her eyes met mine and I knew what I had to do.

"Same here. Bye, Jess."

I hit End on my phone. I wanted more than anything to push Liza against the wall and make her mine. I wanted what should have been mine. But I did what we both needed me to do. When I let go of her arm, the look in her eyes about killed me. She was about to say something when I turned and walked away from her.

The next thing I heard was the door opening and Mrs. Jenkins saying, "Good morning, Liza. Are y'all ready to head to Mr. McMurphy's?"

"Yes. The sooner we get there, the better. I'll be down in the truck, Walker."

I pulled my T-shirt over my head and grabbed my bag as I made my way to the door, mumbling curses under my breath.

Layton walked around one of the three horses I'd pulled aside. His hands moved along the horse as his eyes took in every detail. I peeked over to Liza, who watched her father intently. I'd spent a few hours this morning with Mr. McMurphy, asking about the three horses that had caught my eye when we'd first walked into the barn. Liza and I had taken two out and worked them each for a few minutes. We didn't speak unless it had to do with the horses. The drive to the ranch had been brutally quiet.

Layton stood up and nodded. He winked at Liza, and she looked at me and smiled. I didn't know if that was a good sign or not. Layton handed the horse off to the stable boy and said, "Tell Mr. McMurphy that all three horses will need to be prepared for travel."

"What?" I said.

Liza skipped and ran over, throwing herself into me. I instinctively wrapped my arms around her, but I was looking at Layton. He gave me this goofy smile as he came over. Liza squeezed me harder, as if this was the last time we'd ever be in each other's arms.

"I'm so proud of you, Walker. You did it." She whispered in my ear.

She pulled back and licked her lips, then blinked slowly before leaning in to kiss me on the cheek. I wanted to take her face in my hands and kiss her properly. When she pulled back, our eyes caught, and I couldn't pull myself from her stare.

"Thank you," I said, my voice struggling to get the words out. Layton walked up and hit me on the back. I quickly turned and smiled at him.

"You're old man is going to be one hell of a proud dad when I tell him you picked out the next three winners." Layton said as he shook my hand.

I didn't know what to say. My whole life, all I ever wanted was to be a part of the ranch, work next to Layton, help my father with the racing side of the business, and marry Liza.

*Wait. What?*

I smiled bigger and returned Layton's handshake. It was all I could do not to jump up and down and yell like a kid. Yep, I was that excited. I'd done it. I'd proved my worth.

Layton turned to Liza. "I say we should all get dinner tonight to celebrate."

Liza was about to answer her dad when Mr. McMurphy walked over, chuckling.

"I knew when the boy pulled out those three horses that you had a natural on your hands, Layton," Mr. McMurphy said, winking at me. He was dressed in the rancher's uniform of jeans, boots, and a button-down. His white cowboy hat looked like it had seen better days.

Layton seemed to be beaming with pride. Liza stood off to the side with a smile as big as the Grand Canyon. I'd never felt so happy in my life.

Layton nodded and said, "I knew he had it in him. He used to follow his daddy and me all over the ranch back home. Started asking questions about the horses when he was three. His daddy, Reed, has the gift as well."

"Apple didn't fall far from the tree! Don't forget, I've worked with Reed before. Bastard knows how to drive a hard bargain. He has a way of buying a million dollar horse for two hundred and fifty thousand."

We all laughed as Liza came and stood next to Layton. "I heard y'all saying dinner. How about you be my guest at some fancy-ass party my wife is a part of?

"How fancy?" Layton and I asked at the same time.

Liza giggled and rolled her eyes.

"Semi-formal. Dixion Bourbon Distillery is having a grand opening this evening. It's invite only," Mr. McMurphy said as he raised his eyebrows.

"Sorry, only brought my jeans and T-shirts," Layton said.

An older woman came over and let out a deep, rumbling laugh. Her silver-grey hair was up in a tight bun. She was dressed in jeans, a blue blouse and fancy cowboy boots.

"Nonsense, Layton Morris. You are not getting out of this that easily. Let's all head into town. This may be a small town, but the area is known for all its wedding venues. There's a whole street filled with nothing but fancy dress stores, and even a tux rental place." She turned to Liza. "My daughter is your age, Liza. I'm sure she'd love to go shopping with us for something that you'll probably never wear again and your daddy will bitch about all the way back to Texas."

Liza laughed, then looked at Layton with pleading eyes. "Oh, Daddy. Please? You said this trip was for us. I want to dance with my handsome father."

I smiled knowing that Layton didn't have a chance in hell.

"Taylor Elizabeth Morris. You cannot bribe me with that look any more." Layton said.

I give him ten seconds.

"Daddy...please?" Liza bit her lower lip and threw it up a notch.

Layton looked away as he rolled his eyes. Then he looked at me.

I held up my hands. "Oh no. No way in hell I'm going."

Layton gave me that look. "Shit," I whispered. "I'm going aren't I?"

Layton nodded. I didn't want to look at Liza—I could already feel her stare burning into me.

Mrs. McMurphy clapped her hands together, startling me. "Let's go shopping," she said, lacing her arm with Liza's.

Layton walked next to me, sighing. "This ought to be an interesting evening."

I nodded as I watched Liza walking ahead of me. "Yep. Should be."

# Nine

## Liza

I stood in Lori's bedroom looking at myself in the mirror. Lori was the youngest of the McMurphy clan, with three older sisters and one older brother.

"Oh my, Liza," she said. "Heads are gonna turn this evening when those boys get a look at you."

She came up behind me and stared at me in the mirror. I wore a turquoise cocktail dress that fell just above my knees. The chiffon flowed beautifully and the sweetheart neckline showed just enough cleavage to raise eyebrows, but not enough to have my father trying to cover me up all night. The crystal-beaded waistband added a nice touch.

"Now, can I please talk you out of wearing your cowboy boots and into putting on something a bit more…formal?" Lori asked, winking at me in the mirror.

I looked down at my boots. "But my boots are comfortable."

She handed me a pair of silver pumps and said, "They look great with jeans I'm sure. These? These are what you need to accent those killer legs of yours. Do you run?"

"Nope. I hate running."

"Elliptical?"

I shook my head. "Nope."

She put her hands on her hips and narrowed her eyes at me. "Stair climber?"

"Um…I ride horses a lot and I love to walk."

She pursed her lips and said, "I officially hate you now."

We both busted out laughing as I slipped the silver shoes on. I had my hair piled on top of head with a few curls falling loose. I had to admit I looked good. I took a picture of myself and sent it to Keith. Next time he got a signal, he'd have something to look at.

Lori and I walked down the stairs of her parent's house and rounded the corner to the main living room. Of course, the first person I saw had to be Walker. He had on jeans that should really not be allowed to be on his body with how perfect they made his ass look, a light blue button down dress shirt, and a cowboy hat to round it all off.

Lori leaned over and whispered, "God, that stubble is hot! Hell, *he's* hot. Look at his eyes with that cowboy hat on!"

I slowly nodded. I was fucked.

Walker plus cowboy hat equals Liza wet between the legs.

I started chewing my lip. I bet his blue button-down brought out the color in his eyes. My phone buzzed so I pulled it out of the little blue clutch purse Lori had leant me. I smiled when I saw that it was Keith. I couldn't wait to see what thought of the dress.

**Keith**: *Where is your engagement ring?*

My heart dropped as I stared at the text message. I'd taken off the ring when Walker and I were working the horses. It was still in Walker's glove box. *Shit! How the hell do you forget about your engagement ring being in another man's glove box? Wait. Nothing about this conversation in my head is making sense!*

**Me**: *I was working some horses and took it off. I just forgot to put it back on.*

**Keith**: *So, in other words, you're going out without your ring.*

I sighed. *Bastard.* My phone immediately began to ring and my father,

Walker, Mr. McMurphy, and Lori's fiancé, Robert, all turned and stared. My father smiled, but what I really noticed was Walkers jaw dropping. I had to admit, I liked that the dress had that much of an impact on him. Our eyes met and I smiled slightly. His eyes widened and he smiled back. I hadn't even noticed that my phone had stopped ringing. As Walker came over to me, I couldn't help but notice his eyes moving up and down my body. When he stopped, they landed right on that perfect amount of cleavage.

"My eyes are up here, Mr. Moore." I said, barely above a whisper.

The way he was looking at me had my body kicking into over drive. I felt like I needed to step into a freezer to cool the hell off. He was about to say something when my phone rang again, making me jump. It was Keith…again.

"Shit! I need to answer this. I'm so sorry." I said as Walker barely nodded his head.

"Um…hello?"

"Liza? Where's the ring?" Keith's voice sounded distant. Cold.

"Hello to you, too, Keith. I'm about to put it back on. I'm sorry. I didn't notice it wasn't on."

Walker immediately looked down at my left hand. If he thought I didn't notice his grin, he was wrong.

"If it meant anything to you, Liza, you wouldn't forget to put it back on."

The hurt in his voice about knocked me over. This wasn't the person I wanted to be. Wearing one man's ring while in love with another.

"It was a simple mistake. I'm still getting used to it." I said as I turned away from Walker. I felt the warmth disappear as Walker walked away from me, heading outside.

*Damn it.* I shook my head to clear my thoughts. Soon he'd be asking Jessica to marry him—I didn't need to be worried about him hearing me talk to Keith.

"Will you put it back on before you go out tonight? And where are you going, anyway? Who's going with you? Is Walker going out with you?"

I sighed heavily, frustrated. "Where are *you*? How come you have a signal? Do you realize you haven't even said if you liked the dress? If you think I look nice in it?"

"Liza, baby I'm sorry." Keith said.

I glanced over and noticed that my father was watching me. "I'm with my father, remember? We're going to a party and, yes, Walker will be there along with a number of other men. Would you like me to stay home and not go?"

"Yes."

My heart slammed against my chest as I tried to register his response. "Excuse me?"

"I mean *no*. Of course not. It's just that I know men are going to eye fuck the hell out of you in that dress. I wish I was there."

I shook my head in disbelief and spun around to head outside for some fresh air. Opening the door, I ran smack into Walker. He took a few steps back. He must have seen the look on my face—he knew I needed air. But I felt him follow me down the porch.

"I'm with my father and…" I turned to see Walker holding up the engagement ring. My mouth went dry as he reached down for my left hand and began to slide the ring onto my finger. His jaw tightened. Without even looking at me, he turned and walked toward his truck. He got in, started it, and just sat there.

"Is the signal…can't…hear…Liza?"

I couldn't pull my eyes from Walker. He looked so…sad.

"The signal must be going out, Keith. I'll call you tomorrow when we head home. Love you. Bye."

Without even waiting for a response, I hung up. I was about to go over to Walker when everyone came out the door.

My father frowned at me. "Where's Walker?"

I pointed to the truck. Daddy had rented it for Walker and me to drive out here.

"You want to ride with Walker or with me?" my father asked with a slight smile.

"You," I replied a little too quickly.

He nodded and stuck his arm out. I laced my arm through his and walked with him to the truck. It took all of my strength not to look over at Walker.

At the table, I took another sip of whatever my father had put in front of me. Bourbon? I needed this. The more I drank, the less I felt. Walker hadn't bothered to look my way all night. I knew I shouldn't be disappointed. No, I didn't feel disappointed. I felt defeated. Something caught my eye, and I looked up to see Walker dancing with some girl. My nostrils flared as I watched them. *Ugh. She can't even two-step right.*

The waiter walked by and I jumped up. "I'll take another one of…whatever this is."

He smiled politely and said, "I'll bring you one right away, Miss."

I nodded. When the waiter walked away, Walker was standing there. His eyes felt like they were trying to capture my every move.

"You might want to slow down, babe," he said.

I let out a gruff laugh. "I'm not your *babe.*"

He nodded. "No, you're not."

My eyes threatened to tear up. "What do you want, Walker?"

He held out his hand. I stared at it as if he was offering something offensive. But when I looked into his eyes, they softened.

"Dance with me, Liza."

My head was telling me not to take his hand, but my heart seemed to be running the show. I placed my hand in his and Walker took us out onto the dance floor. I took deep breaths, preparing to be close to his body. When I woke this morning to find that Walker had held me all night, I was so pissed that I'd fallen asleep so fast. I'd slept the best I'd slept in months, and I knew why. I was in the arms of the man I'd loved since childhood.

Walker spun me around once and pulled me to him as I laughed.

"Do you remember how good we were together?" He said. When I made a face, he quickly blurted, "I mean how good we *danced* together."

I looked away as I nodded. "I remember," I said, biting the inside of me cheek.

Hunter Hayes song "Storyline" was playing. Walker put his hand on my neck, pulling me closer as we took off two-stepping. It didn't take long for us to fall back into sync. I saw my father talking to a few older men. He did a double-take when he saw Walker and me. I gave him a quick wave.

He smiled and waved back. Then it happened. The fast song stopped, and a slow song began to play. The heavens were not on my side, it seemed.

Jessie Ware's "Say You Love Me" began playing and Walker held me closer to him. I buried my face in his chest. I couldn't bear the thought of looking at him. His touch alone was beginning to bring my defenses down. *Keith. I'm engaged to Keith.* Well...not really. I haven't said yes.

Walker moved his hand softly up and down my back. I sucked in a breath as the craziest feelings zipped through my body. I'd never really gotten over Walker. I'd just pushed my feelings down for so long, convincing myself that I was okay.

I pulled back and looked into Walker's eyes. It was as if the entire room disappeared and it was just the two of us. He gently placed his hand on the side of my face.

"You look so beautiful tonight, Liza. You're absolutely breathtaking. No other woman in this room holds a candle to you."

I tried to hold back a sob. If only Keith had said those words to me.

I tried to talk, but all that came out was an awkward sound. I cleared my throat and whispered, "Thank you. You look...so handsome."

I wanted to reach up and feel his face, rough with stubble. I needed him to touch me so badly that I wanted to cry out. His eyes fell to my lips and I licked them, anticipating the kiss I knew he wanted to share. He slowly leaned in, and I moaned quietly. His lips barely brushed against mine, and I sucked in a breath. "Walker..." I whispered.

"Liza," he said against my lips. "You'll never know how much I wish we hadn't..."

"Walker?"

My father's voice made Walker let go of me. He took a step back as he removed his cowboy hat and pushed his hand through his hair. My breathing was erratic and I felt dizzy. Now we'd almost kissed *twice* in the last two days. And twice we'd been stopped. Fate was stepping in—we both needed to listen.

I swallowed as I turned to see my father. The look in his eyes said it all.

"Taylor, are you ready to head back to the McMurphys'?"

My father only ever called me Taylor when he was upset or disappointed. And he'd just called me Taylor. My eyes darted back to Walker.

He looked like he was about to puke. I knew the last thing he wanted to do was disappoint my father.

"Um…sure," I said.

My father had decided we'd stay this evening instead of traveling back to the resort. I turned and headed for the table. Then it hit me—I'd had a lot of alcohol. *Damn it.*

My father held the truck door open for me as I climbed into the cab. When I glanced out the window, I saw Walker walking to the rental truck. I leaned my head on the seatback and sighed. Daddy got in and shut the door, started the truck, and pulled out. The entire ride back to the ranch was in dead silence. I could feel his questions burning.

When he pulled up and put the truck in park, he dragged in a deep breath. "Liza? I just need to know something."

My lower lip twitched as I tried to hold back tears. I stared straight ahead, watching the lights of Walkers truck as it came down the drive.

"Are you in love with Walker?"

My jaw trembled. "Yes."

"Are you in love with, Keith?"

The tears could no longer be held at bay. I let them fall freely as I turned to my father.

"Not…like…I…I love…Walker." I cried as my father pulled me closer. I buried my face in his chest. "Daddy, please tell me what to do. I don't know what to do. I've never stopped loving him. Please tell me what to do."

"Shh…it's okay, baby girl. I promise you, it's okay."

I couldn't control my tears. It was like three years of pushed down feelings were bubbling up to the surface all at once, breaking free. My father held me, and I cried until I had no tears left.

I'd admitted it. Now what was I going to do about it?

# Ten

## Walker

Three weeks had passed since the Kentucky trip. Liza had done everything in her power to avoid me. I couldn't blame her. Twice I'd almost kissed her, making both of us break promises to people we cared about.

I was attempting to repair a fence, and my built up frustrations were starting to peak. When the wire snapped, I picked up my hammer and yelled as I threw it as far as I could.

"Do you feel better?"

I whirled around to see Layton. His arms were crossed over his chest and he had a smirk on his face. I'd been waiting for him to talk to me about what had happened in Kentucky, but he had yet to bring it up.

I shook my head. "No, sir. Not at all. I'd like to beat the shit out of something." Dropping my hands to my knees I took deep breaths. "No...everything is fucked up."

Layton placed his hand on my back. "Let's go for a ride."

I stood and watched him walk back to his truck. I slowly followed. It felt like I was walking in thick mud, fighting to take every step. When I got into the truck, I waited for him to start talking. When he began driving in silence, I decided to keep my mouth shut. The longer I could put off hearing how disappointed he was, the better.

Layton pulled up and parked. I looked around.

"You brought me to where you and Whitley got married?"

Layton smiled and nodded. "Sure did. Come on."

He got out of the truck and made his way down the sidewalk. When we came to the gazebo, he stared at it.

He cleared his throat. "Sometimes, we want nothing more than to go back in time. Change a time or place that something happened. Change what happened altogether."

I nodded, looking at the gazebo where I'd first told Liza I loved her. It was the night before leaving for college, and I'd given her the ring that she now wore around her neck. I knew she didn't think I noticed, but I could see it under her shirt every day.

Layton walked up the steps, sat down, and looked at me. He gestured for me to sit across from him.

*Oh shit. Here we go.* I slowly made my way up and sat down. I didn't want to look him in the eyes, but what kind of man would that make me?

"How is Jessica?"

Ugh. He was going in for the kill.

I swallowed. "She's good. She's um...she's back in town. I would have gone to see her, but she asked me to give her a day to get rested up."

Layton cocked his head at me. "Really? I would think she would be eager to see you."

I shrugged. "I guess I didn't think about it like that."

"And you—you're not eager to see her?"

I was about to answer, but I stopped myself. It hit me like a brick wall. "I have to tell her. It's not fair to her. Not when I love Liza."

The corner of Layton's mouth rose in a slight smile. Like he was glad I'd figured it out on my own. I didn't need him to beat it into me. I looked down to the ground and then back at him. "Did you know when you sent us to the McMurphys'?"

He nodded. "Yes."

I stared at him. "I figured out that you'd given Liza the address to the bed and breakfast. Did you know we'd get lost?"

He let chuckled. "I know you two. I knew you'd argue about getting lost. I also knew where you were, because the truck wasn't really a rental.

It was a friend of mine's truck, and he has a GPS tracker on it to keep track of his sixteen-year-old son."

I laughed. "No shit. Mrs. Jenkins?"

"Told her where to find y'all."

I shook my head. A million different things were running through my head. "What if Liza and I had ended up sleeping together that night?"

I saw the muscles in Layton's jaw tighten. "I was willing to take that chance. There's one thing I know for certain about you, Walker. You're a gentleman. I don't think you'd allow yourself or Liza to become cheaters. When I saw the two of you dancing together, I knew for certain. I wasn't sure if you'd stop yourselves or not, so I stepped in."

I looked down as my heart beat faster. "I'm glad you did. I wish I was that sure of myself, sir. I love her. Just being around her can be a struggle. I've had to stop myself a million times from telling her I love her and...well, um...from telling her I—"

He held up his hand. "I get what you're saying. Stop torturing yourselves—and me."

I pushed out a breath and said, "I can't stand the thought of her being with another man. But if she truly loves him, and that is what she wants, I'll stand back and let her live the life she wants."

Layton didn't respond for a few minutes. "What are you going to do son?"

I closed my eyes. "Well, one thing I know is that I have to talk to Jessica."

Layton nodded. "Walker, I brought you here because a lot of memories—good and bad—happened in this very spot. You can't go back to the night that you decided to break up. Everything happens for a reason, son. Every road you travel down is because of a decision you made. Some decisions are good, some are bad. Learn from each one. But don't look back in regret. Always look forward in anticipation of what could still be."

I smiled at the man who was like a second father to me. I stood and Layton followed.

"Thank you, sir. Thank you for helping to guide me down the right road."

"I'm always here for you, Walker. I love you like a son."

I checked the time on my phone. "Jessica should be home by the time I get to her house. I'm going to just head on into Austin and talk to her."

"I think that is the best thing to do." Layton shook my hand and pulled me in for a hug. When he pulled back, he winked at me. "Just remember one thing. Don't sit back and let Liza walk away because you think you're doing what's best for her."

I nodded. "Yes, sir. I'll remember that."

Layton smiled and slapped me on the back. He and my father liked doing that. Sometimes, I swear, they hit a hell of a lot harder than need be.

"Come on, son. Let's head on back and fix that fence so you can head to Austin."

I pulled up and parked in front of Jessica's house. I was about to text her when I noticed a BMW parked in the driveway. I stared at it for the longest time. *Why did it look so familiar?*

**Me**: *Hey. What are you doing?*

A good two minutes passed before she responded.

**Jessica**: *Just about to lay down and take a nap. I'm wiped out. All that traveling just sucked.*
**Me**: *Are your parents' home?*
**Jessica**: *No. Just little ol' me wishing I had your body close.*
**Me**: *Is that right?*
**Jessica**: *I can't wait to see you. I'm excited about the adventure we're about to take. I'm tired of getting myself off and being alone. I want you, baby.*

Opening the door to my truck, I got out and made my way up the driveway. I glanced at the BMW and shook my head. I knew where Jessica's parents kept the spare key. I made my way around the side of the house to the small potted plant that held the ugliest plant I'd ever seen. Jessica's dad said no one in their right mind would even think to look under that plant for a key. Lifting the pot I stuck my hand under it until I felt the cool metal of the key.

I walked back to the front of the house and prayed like hell that she hadn't set the alarm as I unlocked the door and slowly opened it. Closing it quietly behind me, I made my way up the stairs and to Jessica's bedroom. It didn't take long to hear her moaning. Then she started calling out.

"Yes. Oh, God! Harder. Give it to me harder!"

I closed my eyes and reached for the door. Slowly, I pushed it open and was stunned by what I saw. I was watching Mitchell Cunningham fuck my girlfriend. I cleared my throat, but with the two of them moaning and going at it like wild animals, they couldn't hear me. I saw one of Jessica's flip-flops nearby. She always wore flip-flops. Everywhere. It drove me fucking nuts. I picked it up and threw it as hard as I could, hitting Mitchell in the head.

"What the fuck? What's going…" He turned and saw me leaning on the doorjamb. "Fuck!" He yelled as he jumped up, covered his dick, and searched for his pants.

"Baby what's wrong?" Jessica turned to see what Mitchell was seeing. The second she saw me, she flew up. "Oh my God. Walker? What…I mean…how did you get in here? I mean…why are you here?"

I raised an eyebrow, remaining silent.

"It's not what you think," she said.

I chuckled. "Really, Jessica? 'Cause I'm thinking my girlfriend is fucking another man. How long has it been going on?"

Mitchell looked to Jess, waiting for her to lead him in the lies they were about to tell.

"Walker, baby, can we just talk in private? I swear to you, Mitchell doesn't mean anything to me. He's just a fuck. That's it."

I glanced at Mitchell. "The night we saw each other at Lunckenbach, you'd been with her that day, hadn't you?"

Jessica spun around and looked at Mitchell. "What? What day? What night are you talking about?"

Mitchell looked away as he barely said, "Yes."

I turned back to Jessica. "How long have you been cheating on me?"

She swallowed hard. Then I saw the tears sliding down her face. "I don't love him. I love *you*. But, being with him feels right. I've been so freaked out about moving to the country and starting this whole new life and..."

I closed my eyes and said, "How. Long. Have. You. Cheated. On. Me?"

"About ten months," she said.

My heart dropped. I shook my head. "Okay."

She cocked her head and let out a nervous giggle. "Okay?"

I looked at Mitchell and then back to her. "Yeah. Okay."

She smiled. "So you...you forgive me?"

I laughed. "Fuck, no! But it just makes my decision so much easier. I was so worried I was about to hurt you. And here you've been cheating on me for ten months."

Her lower lip jutted out and she stumbled on her words. "Wh...what decision?"

"I came here to break it off with you."

Her eyes widened. "What? Why?" It must have all clicked in that brief moment our eyes locked. "It's because of her isn't it? You've never stopped loving her have you?"

I shook my head. "No, I never did. In a way, I guess that doesn't make me any better than you."

I turned and began walking out into the hallway. I felt her grab my arm.

"Wait, Walker. We can work this out. Maybe you could move to Austin and work for Daddy. I know we can work this out."

I pushed her off of me. "No. I don't love you, Jessica. I thought I did, but I realize now that I never loved you. I settled for you."

Her jaw dropped and she went to slap me but I stepped back. Mitchell was standing in the doorway, watching. I turned to him and said, "Good luck dude, you're gonna need it."

As I made my way out of the house, I tossed the spare key on the table by the front door. It felt like the weight of a hundred elephants had been lifted from my shoulders.

On my drive back to Llano, I tried to figure out what to do next. I wasn't sure if I should tell Liza I loved her or not. I wasn't sure what she'd do about Keith. I knew she didn't love him enough to leave her family. I knew that, deep in her heart, there were so many reasons she wanted to stay in Llano. I prayed to God I was one of those reasons.

# Eleven

## Liza

A month had passed since I'd talked to Walker. I'd seen him plenty of times, but he didn't know I was there. It was a bit pathetic on my part, really—sneaking around to get a glimpse of him. My father kept asking me if I'd talked to Walker about my true feelings. But I couldn't bring myself to do it. I knew he was with Jessica. And I had Keith.

Leaning against the barn stall, I sighed. Keith hadn't texted or called in almost a week. I wasn't worried but, then again, I was. I knew he'd be back next week, and I'd have to give him an answer. I wasn't ready. I needed more time to think. To understand my feelings. I stood up and walked back to the tack room. What I needed was a ride.

I was walking Tiny out of the barn when I stopped suddenly. Walker was headed straight for me. *Shit. Shit. Shit.* I turned Tiny and began walking him the opposite way.

"Liza!"

"No," I said under my breath as I walked faster. "I'm not ready to see you."

"Liza!" Walker called out. He whistled and Tiny stopped on a dime, about pulling my arm out of its socket. "Traitor," I whispered as Tiny jerked his head.

Walker ran up. "Hey! Long time, no see."

I smiled politely and nodded. "I was about to go for a ride, so…"

"Want some company?"

I stepped back and said, "No." What I wanted to tell him was that I couldn't think straight when I was around him.

His eyes filled with hurt. "Oh, um, okay. We just haven't seen each other and—"

"I can't…I can't keep doing this."

His eyes became something I'd never seen before. "Doing what?"

I pointed to the space between us. "This. Us, I mean. Keith deserves more than this. I'm…I'm…well, I'm going to be moving to Dallas with him."

I watched as Walker's face dropped. "Why?"

I laughed. "Why? Well, because we're going to get married. Maybe. And that's what couples do. I need you stay away because when we're together I…"

I watched as the muscles in his neck flexed. He took a step closer to me, making me take a step back, smacking into Tiny's side.

"I need to stay away from you…why?"

I swallowed hard. "You *know* why." I said, narrowing my eyes at him.

Walker took another step toward me. "No, Liza, I don't know why."

He was inches away and I could feel the heat between us. "I can't do this, Walker. Please don't make me do this."

"Do what, Liza?"

"Walk away from us again."

He took another step closer and put his lips to my ear. "Don't walk away, then. Stay."

*Stay.*

I closed my eyes and put my hands on his chest. His warmth raced through my body.

"Walker, I—"

The moment his lips smashed against mine, something happened. I lost all sense of reality and let my heart take the lead. My hands moved up and around his neck. He lifted me up and I wrapped my legs around him as our tongues explored each other. It had been forever since I'd been kissed like this—since the last time Walker kissed me.

"Oh, God," I whispered as we broke for air.

My hands were in his hair as I pulled him to my lips. Walker walked us to the barn and into an empty stall. He pushed me up against the wood and the pain both excited and scared me. He reached a side of me that I didn't understand. He slipped his hand into my shirt, pushing up my bra. He twisted and pulled my nipple as I moaned into his mouth.

"Liza, I need you," Walker whispered behind my ear. "Please, stay."

The engagement ring caught my eye. Oh. God. What was I doing?

Walker set me down and began pushing his hand into my riding pants. *Stop this Liza. Keith. Think about Keith.*

But maybe I could have just one touch. I only needed one touch to sooth the ache.

His hand slipped into my panties and I let out whimper. I needed him to touch me just once more. His fingers moved across my sensitive skin until they finally found where I needed relief. I lifted my leg as Walker pushed two fingers inside of me and let out a moan. Then he stopped. He pulled his hand out and took a step back. I shook my head.

"Wait...what are you doing? Don't stop!" I said.

"I need to know what you're going to do, Liza, before we continue this."

My head was spinning and I longed for his touch. My head slowly started to take control back from my heart.

I reached under my shirt and adjusted my bra. "This is what I mean. I lose all control when you're around. I can't tell you no." I pushed him.

He was stunned. "What are you saying, Liza?"

I felt tears building in my eyes. "I've made a promise to someone, Walker. I'm wearing the ring he gave me."

Walker pulled my necklace out from under my shirt. "What about this ring, Liza?"

I swallowed. My heart was breaking in two and I didn't know what to do. "Walker, please. Please don't do this to me. I'm begging you. What about Jessica?"

Walker dropped the ring and it fell against my chest. "I'm not with Jessica."

I sucked in a breath of air. "Why?"

Walker backed away. "I broke up with her."

I shook my head and looked into his eyes. "Walker, why?"

He began to walk out of the stall, but looked back at me to say, "I couldn't be with her when I was in love with someone else."

My mouth fell open and I stood there, frozen in place.

"You'd better get Tiny," Walker said. "He's starting to wander off."

Walker left the barn. I tried to call to him, but all that came out were sobs. I fell to the ground and whispered his name over and over. It had happened again. I watched as the only man I'd ever truly loved walked away, leaving me alone and broken.

I jumped up when Reed walked in. "Any sign of him?" I asked.

Reed shook his head. "No, sweetheart. Nothing."

I sat back down as Courtney wrapped an arm around me. "Liza, I'm sure Walker is fine. We just need to stay calm."

I nodded as Ava walked up and handed me a hot chocolate. I smiled weakly at her.

"I know how much you love hot chocolate so…" she trailed off.

Ava sat down on the sofa opposite of her mother and me. Her phone pinged and she grabbed it, quickly typing back to someone. She stood up and walked to the kitchen.

I took a sip of the hot chocolate and turned to Courtney. "I'm sorry, I'm the reason he left without telling anyone. This is all my fault."

Courtney shook her head and gave me that sweet smile of hers. "No, don't say that, Liza. Whatever happened between you and Walker is between you—"

"He's okay."

Reed, Courtney, and I all turned to Ava.

"What?" I asked, my hands shaking. Ava had been texting Walker.

"That was Walker. He just sent me a text. He's with Jase."

I stood up. *Jase?* "What do you mean?"

Ava rolled her eyes. "Jase has that internship in Austin, remember? I guess Walker went to stay a few days with him. Told me to tell Layton and Dad that he was sorry he left without saying anything, and that he'd be home tomorrow."

I let out the breath I had been holding in. "He's coming home? Tomorrow?"

Ava nodded. "Um, Liza, he didn't want me to tell you, but I couldn't do that to you."

Courtney stood and kissed Ava on the cheek. "You did right, telling Liza." Courtney turned to me, taking my mug. "Let's take you home sweetheart, you looked exhausted."

As I walked to my car, everything was muffled. Courtney and Reed were talking. Courtney would drive me, and Reed would follow. I sat in the passenger seat with my eyes closed until Courtney said we'd arrived. In the house, I made my way upstairs to my room. Collapsing on my bed, I stared at the ceiling with no tears left to cry. When I heard a knock at the door, I didn't even have the energy to tell whoever it was to come in. The door opened and my mother came in. From the corner of my eye I saw something in her hand—my phone. I must have left it at home when I'd rushed over to Walker's house.

"Uh, honey? Keith has been trying to call you for the last hour."

I groaned and rolled over. My mother set the phone on the bedside table. I closed my eyes and thought about the night in Kentucky when Walker had held me so I could sleep.

"Walker..." I whispered as exhaustion finally took over.

I lifted my arm and ran it across my forehead, wiping away the sweat that was threatening to burn my eyes again. "Mom, it's so hot out here. Why do y'all do this?"

Courtney laughed.

"Oh, wait. Do you have your handy-dandy snake shotgun nearby,

Court?" My mother asked.

Courtney walked over to the porch and pulled a shotgun down. "Hell, yes, I do."

We all giggled and I rolled my eyes. My mother and I had gone over to Walker's parents' house to help Courtney with her overly extravagant garden.

"I thought the garden was Reed's deal." I said, as I sat on my ass and sighed.

Courtney smiled at me. "I thought you loved working in the garden, Liza. Enjoy this now, because I'm sure you won't have it in Dallas."

Her words stung instantly and her smiled dropped.

"Oh, honey. I wasn't meaning anything…"

I held up my hand and gave her a smile. Looking around, my heart dropped when I saw the tree house. I thought about the countless hours Walker and I had spent up there. First as best friends, then as something more. I closed my eyes and thought about the time we'd almost made love. Maybe if we had, we'd never have walked away from each other.

*The movie no longer held my attention as I watched Walker. I loved his scruffy beard. He laughed at something on the screen and then looked at me. His blue eyes pierced mine with a seductive glance. It made my insides all kinds of crazy. His eyes fell to my lips, and I ran my tongue along my teeth. He moved over me and I slid down so that he could rest on top. He pushed his hard dick against me and I moaned. It wasn't long before my pants were off. Soon he made me come with his expert fingers. The only reason we could fool around in the tree house was because both of our parents were in Austin at some function.*

*"Tell me how far, Liza," Walker whispered against my ear. "I want you so much, but I need you to tell me, baby."*

*"Make love to me, Walker. Please."*

*"Liza, I wanted our first time to be…"*

*Walker stopped talking and turned his head. "Did you hear that?"*

*I bit my lip and nodded. "Someone's here."*

*Walker stood up and pulled up his jeans. He walked over to the window and then spun around. "Get dressed, Liza. My parents are back!"*

"Want to tell me what has you smiling over there so big?" My mother asked, pulling me from my thoughts.

I grinned and I shook my head. "Nothing, just an old memory."

Courtney laughed. "It must have been a happy one with the way you're smiling."

I looked back toward the tree house and said, "Yeah, it was."

I felt a hand on my shoulder. My mother knelt down and smiled. "Do you love him?"

My eyes darted over to Courtney, who was giving me that look. Like she thought I knew something and wasn't sharing it.

"Who?"

"If you're really asking me that, Liza, then this talk is long overdue."

My heart was beating harder. "What does that mean, Mom? You could be talking about anyone. Jase, Dad, Keith…"

"Walker," she whispered as she looked at me intently.

I looked away. No one said anything for a few minutes and, when Courtney came and sat down on the ground next to me, it was all I could do to hold back my tears.

"When I first met Reed, I swear it was love at first sight."

I looked into her eyes. "Was it?" I asked.

She chuckled. "Oh yes, it was. The moment he looked at me, my body turned to Jell-O. But I fought it like hell."

I cocked my head and asked, "Why?"

My mother and Courtney shared a look. "It's a long story that someday we'll talk about. Let's just say that I pushed my feelings down for so long that I started to feel like I was losing myself."

I knew the feeling.

Courtney let out a sigh and said, "Sweetheart. You've always talked about your dreams, what you wanted. I know dreams change, and plans change. But when a guy slips a ring on your finger, you really shouldn't need months to think about your answer."

I could feel my lower lip trembling. I blinked slowly and felt hot tears running down my cheeks as I glanced over to my mom. "I don't want to hurt either one of them, Mom."

She nodded. "It's not just about them, Taylor. This is also about you. Who do *you* want to be with? Who's arms do you want to wake up in every morning?"

I already knew that answer. I was about to say so when we heard someone coming down the driveway. Courtney looked up and smiled. She started walking toward the driveway. I wiped away my tears and stood up. I smiled when I saw Walker's truck.

My mother put her arm around me and pulled me closer as she whispered, "I knew he couldn't stay in Austin that much longer." I laughed as I wiped another tear away. I looked back at the truck and noticed someone in the passenger seat.

"Who's with him? That's not Jase."

The sun was hitting Walker's windshield just enough to hide the person in the passenger seat. The truck parked and my mother and I walked toward it. The closer we got, the better I could see. My breath caught. I couldn't believe this was happening.

Walker got out of his truck and shut the door. He looked directly at me, even though his mother was walking toward him. I could hardly breathe. He was wearing his backwards baseball cap with jeans and a tight A&M T-shirt. My desire for him bloomed in my stomach.

"Look who I found at your house when I stopped by to talk, Liza," Walker said.

Keith stepped out of Walker's truck.

"Oh, shit," my mother said, holding me closer.

"Keith," I whispered as he smiled at me.

I glanced back at Walker. His mother was saying something to him, but his eyes were glued on me. I'd wanted nothing more than to run into his arms less than a minute ago. Now my feet felt cemented to the ground. Keith seemed confused as to why I was just standing there. I went to talk, but nothing would come out.

"Liza?" My mother said, giving me a friendly push in no particular direction.

I started to take a step, but stopped.

Keith laughed. "Are you that shocked to see me, baby?" he asked.

He took me into his arms and spun me around. When he set me down, he cupped my face in his hands and kissed me gently. I wanted to feel that familiar feeling building in my belly when he touched me, but there was nothing.

When he pulled his lips from mine, he whispered, "I've missed you so much, baby."

My eyes teared up as he smiled and pulled me to him. I couldn't help but look at Walker. He just stared. Courtney placed her hand on his arm and said something to him as he nodded. He turned and walked toward the back of his house. I couldn't help crying.

Keith held me closer and said, "It's okay, baby, I'm here now."

# Twelve

## Walker

My father sat down at the bar stool next to me as I downed my beer. I wasn't in the mood for a lecture.

"Hey," my dad said, nudging my shoulder with his.

I didn't bother looking at him as I set my empty bottle down. "Hey," I muttered.

"I thought I might find you here," my father said, waving the bartender down and ordering a Bud Light.

I laughed, irritated. "What made you think I'd be at Joe's Bar, dad?" I asked.

The bartender set his beer down and turned to me. "Want another one, handsome?"

I winked at her. "Why the hell not? I have nowhere else I need to be."

She licked her top lip. "I'm off in an hour. I bet I can find somewhere to go."

I laughed and nodded. "I think I like the sound of that plan."

"Excuse me? Want to go grab that beer now?" my father asked her.

She winked at me, turned, and headed to get my beer.

My father cleared his throat and said, "I knew you'd be here because it's like looking in a damn mirror. I've been right where you are, son. Believe me—drinking doesn't really make the pain go away."

The bartender set the beer down, accompanied by a piece of paper with her name and number on it. I gave her a sexy smile.

I took a swig of beer and turned to my father. "Well, if beer doesn't make it go away, maybe fucking a hot bartender will."

My father glared at me. "You're an asshole when you drink, Walker."

I went to say something but his stare was intense. I knew I wasn't drunk enough to get away with insulting my own father.

"Have you talked to Liza?"

I laughed and took another swig of beer. "Nope. If you hadn't noticed, her fiancé is in town, and they seemed anxious to get reacquainted."

My father lifted his beer and took a drink. "I think you should call her."

I closed my eyes. "Why, Dad? So she can reject me again? Tell me how she's starting a new life with Keith. Maybe she wants to tell me all about packing up and moving away from everyone who cares about her. Moving away from her dreams. From…"

"Say it, Walker."

I shook my head. "Doesn't fucking matter anymore."

My father grabbed my arm and turned me toward him. "Say. It."

"Me! There! I said it! She's moving away from me, Dad. Walking away from…us."

"Then go tell her how you feel."

"I was going to. That's why I was at her house. I was going to ask her to stay here, with me, but I was too late. She picked *him* dad. She picked him."

I drank the rest of my beer before slamming the bottle onto the counter. "I just need to forget and move on. Find someone who will…" I swallowed. "Who will love me."

My father let out a gruff laugh. "Because Liza doesn't? Is that what you think, Walker? You think she doesn't love you? You're wrong. I see the way she looks at you. Everyone sees it, son. She doesn't look at this Keith guy that way."

I turned to my father. We looked so much alike. My father was even wearing a backwards baseball cap. "I need to be alone, Dad. Just for tonight, I need to be alone."

My father glanced back over to the hot bartender. "Don't do anything you'll regret, son. I'm telling you that from experience."

He stood up and threw a couple twenties onto the bar and squeezed my shoulder. He slapped the hell out of my back and headed out the door.

An hour later, I found myself leaving the bar with a blonde. I had no idea what her name was.

"Follow me home, handsome?"

I nodded and jumped into my truck. I followed her to a small brick house about five blocks from Joe's. Pulling into her driveway, I parked behind her car. She motioned for me to follow her. Unlocking her front door, she reached in and turned on a light. I followed in and shut the door. Before I could say anything, she pushed me against the door and kissed me as her hand made its way to my dick and squeezed.

"Oh, *hell* yeah," she said as she pulled her lips away and quickly pulled her shirt over her head. I checked out her chest. Her tits were practically falling out of a bra that was clearly too small for her. I cupped her breast as she tipped her head back. Moving my lips to her neck, I kissed her and pushing up her bra up, letting her breasts fall free. I moved my lips down to her nipple and sucked on it—hard. Her little moans made my dick jump.

"That's it," she murmured as she turned and pressed her ass against my dick. "I want it from behind, and I want it hard and fast." She pushed off of me and walked into her living room.

I took off my baseball cap and ran my hand through my hair. Placing my cap back on, I glanced around. The walls were tan and there was hardly any furniture in the place. She had a small sofa and coffee table. Nothing else. *What the fuck am I doing?*

I reached for the doorknob as she called out, "I have condoms if you don't have one."

Rolling my eyes, I opened the door and didn't look back as I made my way to my truck. What I needed was to get out of Llano for a few days.

Back in my truck, I called the only person I knew I could count on to help me.

# Thirteen

## Liza

Sitting at my kitchen table, I stared at Keith, listening to him go on and on about his damn hiking trip with his father. He'd assumed I'd cried because I'd been happy to see him. I glanced at my father, and he looked bored out of his mind. I knew that deep down inside he was praying I wouldn't marry Keith.

My mother raised an eyebrow at me and tilted her head toward Keith.

I nodded to let her know I got the hint. I needed to talk to Keith. I needed to tell him we were over. I needed to tell him I was in love with another man.

My father looked at me with pleading eyes. I couldn't help but giggle. I finally stood and placed my hand on Keith's shoulder. He turned and met my gaze.

"Keith, can we step outside and sit on the porch? I need to talk to you."

Keith's smile faded. He turned to my parents and said, "If you'll excuse us."

My mother and father both nodded.

Keith took my hand as we walked out and onto the back porch. I pointed to the pool and we made our way to a table. Keith pulled a chair out for me. Sitting down, I looked up at the clear sky. The stars were probably the brightest I'd seen them in a long time.

"Thank you," I said.

He walked around the table and sat across from me. I took a deep breath and was about to speak when Keith laughed and said, "Jesus, I've been waiting hours to be alone with you and *this* is where you want to talk?" He used air quotes around the word "talk."

I looked away. I'd been trying to figure out how to do this ever since he'd arrived.

I turned back to face Keith. He was staring at me, concerned. He finally chuckled.

"Keith, there isn't an easy way for me to say this."

Shaking his head he said, "Don't do this, Liza."

I chewed on my lip and stared at the ring on my finger. I slipped it off and tried to talk. When nothing came out, I cleared my throat and wiped my tears. "I never wanted to hurt you, Keith. But I think I've always known that my place was here, in Llano."

He closed his eyes and shook his head. "You're not marrying me because you want to stay in this town? You're really picking Llano over me, Liza?"

I swallowed and sucked in a shaky breath. "No, I'm not marrying you because I'm…I'm…" A sob escaped my throat and I placed a hand over my mouth.

"What? You're what?"

I closed my eyes and counted to five as I tried to catch my breath. When I opened my eyes, I extended my hand to him, offering back the ring.

"My heart belongs here, too. I'm in love with someone else. I've always been in love with him. I'll always be in love with him. It's not fair to you for me to keep pretending."

Keith looked away for a few seconds and quickly wiped away a tear. He didn't bother to look at me as he asked, "Walker?"

I whispered, "Yes."

His head snapped back to me. "Did you ever love me, Liza?"

I gasped. "Of course I did. I just…I mean…I…"

He smiled, but the muscles in his neck were flexed. "You loved him more."

I couldn't speak. My mouth went dry. Deep in my heart I always knew Keith was not the guy I wanted to spend the rest of my life with.

Keith took the ring from me, got up, and walked around the table to stand in front of me. "I could've given you the world. Anything you wanted, you would've had. I hope you won't look back and realize this was the biggest mistake of your life, Liza."

I was briefly taken aback. Shaking my head I said, "The biggest mistake of my life was walking away from him in the first place." I stood up and looked into his eyes. "I'm sorry, Keith. I never meant to hurt you."

He placed his hand on my face and whispered, "I'm sorry, too. He'll never love you like I love you. You'll soon see that." He brushed his thumb along my cheek before dropping his hand, turning, and walking away. He quickly got in his car and drove off.

I sat back down and sighed as I rested my head against the back of the chair, staring up at the night sky. I closed my eyes and a single tear escaped, leaving a hot trail on my cheek. When I opened my eyes, I just watched the sky. Someone pulled out a chair and sat down. I knew it was one of my parents, but I wished like hell that it was Walker. I brought my head forward only to see my brother Jase at the table.

"Did you break up with Keith?" He asked as he messed around with a twig.

I nodded. "Yeah, I did."

He took a deep breath as he sat back in his chair. "I never did like that guy."

I giggled and looked away. I wasn't sure why I laughed—my heart felt heavy. But I wasn't sure if it was because of what had happened with Keith or if it was the haunting look in Walker's eyes earlier this afternoon.

"What are you doing here?" I asked, reaching for his hand.

He smiled and I couldn't help but smile back. He had the most amazing smile. His dark hair and blue eyes made him a mini version of my father. Jase had a sensitive heart. He cared so much about people, and I wanted him to find him a girl who would make him see the man he really was.

He rubbed his thumb back and forth across my hand. "I came to tell you that Walker was going to leave Llano."

My smile dropped and I sat up straight. "He just came back home, where is he—"

Jase put his fingers up to my mouth and said, "Liza, let me finish please."

I nodded as I leaned back and tried to calm my accelerated heartbeat.

"Walker wanted to leave for a couple of days only. He didn't want to be in town with you and Keith here together. He was pretty messed up, sis, when he called me. He wanted to head to South Padre, but I talked him into the hunting lodge."

I scrunched my eyebrows together and said, "The hunting lodge? Here? On our property?"

Jase smiled and nodded. "Yeah, the one Dad used to take us too to camp out. He always said that was the place where he and mom finally realized they loved each other. I couldn't think of a better place for you and Walker to get your damn shit together."

I jumped up and hugged my brother. "I love you, Jase and I owe you so big for this. Does he know you're telling me?"

Jase laughed. "*Hell* no. He made me swear to keep quiet until you and Keith left. I figured, with the breakup, Walker would be okay with me sharing this with you."

I kissed Jase on the cheek and started toward the ranch Jeep. I was thanking God that my father kept the keys in it all the time. I didn't want to have to go back and tell my parents what had happened and where I was going.

As I started the Jeep, Jase called, "I'll tell Mom and Dad you won't be back tonight!"

I smiled and waved as I took off toward the hunting cabin. My heart felt like it was slamming against my chest. My hands were sweaty and I was trying to remember if I'd shaved my legs this morning. I shook my head to clear my thoughts. I reached down and ran my hand along my leg. Smooth! I did a little fist pump as I drove toward my future.

I didn't want Walker to hear the Jeep, so I parked it about a half a mile down the road. Opening up the glove box, I smiled when I saw a flashlight. My father was obsessed with flashlights, so I never doubted that there would be one in the Jeep to light my way to the cabin. I grabbed the flashlight and hopped out of the Jeep.

I made my way up onto the small porch of the cabin. The lights were all on and I heard music. Putting my ear to the door, I heard "Just a Little Bit of Your Heart" by Ariana Grande playing. I closed my eyes, placing both hands over my mouth to hold back my tears. When I felt my emotions were under control, I turned the doorknob and pushed the door open. I was immediately hit with the smell of a fire burning in the wood stove. I entered the room and found Walker sitting in a chair with his back to the door, watching the fire. The music had covered the sound of the door opening and closing. He hadn't heard me come in.

The hunting cabin barely had any furniture in it. There were two beds with a small dresser next to each one and a small table with two chairs.

Closing my eyes, I placed one hand on my belly, covering my mouth with the other. I loved him so much. I prayed to God I hadn't messed things up. I opened my eyes and dropped my hands. Slowly, I approached him. He sat up straight. He knew I was here. Biting my lip, I walked over and stood in front of him. He looked up at me, and our eyes met. I sucked in a breath. When I saw a tear slide down his cheek, a sob escaped my lips.

"I've always loved you," I said, wiping my tears away and smiling. "I'll love you forever. Only you."

I stood there, waiting for him to say something. When he pulled his mouth into a grin, I couldn't help but grin back.

He blinked slowly as he said, "I can't live without you, Liza."

Dropping to my knees, I laid my head in his lap. "I'm so sorry. Please forgive me. I didn't mean to hurt you, Walker. I was so confused and...and..." I looked up into his eyes. "I've always wanted you. Only you. I was going to tell you today, but then Keith showed up."

He placed his hands on my arms and brought me to him. I sat on his lap and wrapped my arms around his neck as I leaned down and kissed him. The kiss was sweet and gentle, filled with so much love. Walker put his hands on my hips and moaned as I pushed down on his hardness. I rocked against him as he pushed his hand through my hair and pulled me in to deepen the kiss. I could feel the buildup moving through my body. I'd never been able to have an orgasm like this with anyone but Walker. He made my body desire him in ways I couldn't understand. I wasn't sure if I ever would.

I pulled my lips back and looked into his eyes. "Walker. Please make love to me."

He stood up and I wrapped my legs around his waist. He smiled as he moved us to the bed and gently laid me down. My heart beat like I was a virgin. In a way, I was. This was my first time with the man I'd been in love with for my whole life.

He leaned down and placed gentle kisses all over my neck and face. Between each kiss he'd speak: "I. Have. Never. In. My. Life. Loved. Someone. Like. I. Love. You."

For once the tears building in my eyes were happy tears.

"I. Promise. To. Never. Leave. You. Again."

Tears spilled from my eyes as I stroked his cheek and looked into his sparkling blue eyes. "I like that promise."

He pulled his T-shirt over his head as he stood. He unbuttoned his pants and pushed them down, and his hard-on sprung out. My eyes grew big. I chewed on my lower lip as I stared. He was huge. I moved my eyes up his body to see him smiling at me.

"Do you like what you see?"

I nodded and said, "I most certainly do."

I sat up and pulled my T-shirt over my head, glad I had a white lace bra on. Walker sat down and placed his hands on my shoulders, pushing me back to a laying position.

"I want to adore your body," he said.

I swallowed as he unbuttoned my jeans. "Lift," he whispered as he pulled them off of my hips and then down each leg. I rubbed my legs together as he tossed my pants to the side. He looked me over like he was memorizing every square inch of my body. I could almost feel the heat coming from him. I wanted to push my hand into my panties to relieve this insane need to have him inside me.

Walker placed his hand on my leg, moving it up, gently using his fingertips to send chills throughout my body. He licked his lips as he reached my panties. Placing his hand on my abdomen, Walker slipped his thumb just under the waistband. When his hand slid into my panties, my chest heaved with my quickening breath. He lightly brushed my clit, making me arch my back and gasp. Then Walker slid his fingers between the sensitive lips and massaged inside of me, making me thrash my head back and forth. He smiled as he watched my body react to his touch. When he pulled his hand away, I wanted to scream.

"Take off your panties, Liza." He said in a seductive voice.

I quickly sat up and pushed my panties down, kicking them onto the floor. Looking down at his dick, I licked my lips and he moaned.

"Lay back."

I did what he asked. He moved down the bed as I pulled my legs up in anticipation.

"I've always wanted to taste you, baby. I don't think I can wait any longer."

I took a deep breath. "Yes," I whispered as I felt him move between my legs. He ran the side of his face down my legs. I could tell that this was going to rock my world. He was going to...

"Oh God!" I yelled as he buried his face between my legs, sucking on my clit. He pushed his fingers inside of me, and the buildup was instant. I grabbed his hair with both hands. I moved my hips as I felt the orgasm building in the very tips of my toes. I thrashed my head whispering, "Don't...want...to come...yet."

He swirled his tongue and began working it in and out of my body. "Walker. Walker!" I screamed as he moved back to my clit, my orgasm hitting me full on. Grasping the sheets, I yelled out his name. I felt my insides pulsing as my body reeled with one of the most intense orgasms of my life. If I hadn't known any better, I'd swear I'd left my body, gone to heaven, and come back down.

"Holy...crap..." I panted as Walker kissed all around my abdomen. He moved his lips up and sucked on my nipples as I took a fistful of his hair and pulled. We moaned in synch as he reached his hand down and finger-fucked me.

"You're so wet, Liza. I want to bury myself so deep in you that you'll never forget I was there."

My breathing was erratic and I sounded needy, but I didn't care. "Yes. Oh God yes, Walker. Please. I want you so much. I need to feel you."

He moved his mouth up to my neck and kissed me until he found the spot behind my ear that drove me mad. I reached down and stroked his dick. I wanted him inside me. I *needed* him inside me.

"Uh, Liza? I want to come when I'm *inside* you," He breathed into my mouth.

"Then please give me what we both want, Walker," I panted.

He moved over me and teased me with his tip. When he looked into my eyes, I could feel the love passing between us. "I love you, Liza."

I licked my lips, cupping his face in my hands. "I love you, Walker. I love you so much."

As he leaned down to kiss me, he pushed himself into me, making me suck in a breath. He slowly moved in and out as we continued kissing. I'd never in my life felt so loved and wanted. The feeling of him moving inside my body, so slowly, was the most amazing feeling I'd ever experienced.

"I love you," Walker whispered against my lips as he moved faster.

I grabbed onto his ass as I moved my body in perfect rhythm with him. I could feel my build up starting. I wanted us to come at the same time, and I was trying like hell to hold off my orgasm. As Walker's rhythm increased, he looked into my eyes, and something magical happened.

Something I don't think I will ever experience again.

# Fourteen

## Walker

I was trying to hold off coming, but I could see it in Liza's eyes. She was close.

"Liza…"

She bit her lip and moved her hands into my hair and pulled. "Walker…I'm so close."

I pulled out, then pushed in harder.

She moaned. "I'm coming. Walker, I'm coming."

I pulled out and pushed in again, moaning. As I repeated the motion, I could feel her squeezing on my dick. "Liza, baby I'm gonna come."

I slammed my lips into hers and kissed her as I poured myself into her body. I'd never experienced something like this before. The love moving between our bodies as we became one was a moment I'd cherish forever.

When I finally finished, I shifted my bodyweight but stayed inside Liza. I could feel my dick twitching and I had to take a few deep breaths to calm my heart.

Liza ran her fingertips along my unshaven face and smiled. "I've never felt anything so amazing. I love you."

I kissed her nose. "I feel the same way, baby. It was beyond amazing. It was…"

"Magical," we said at the same time.

When we laughed together, she squeezed down on my dick again, and I swear I felt a little rise from him. I was about to pull out of her when it hit me.

Her smile faded and she looked at me, concerned. I'm sure it was in response to the look of terror that was on my face.

"Liza, oh God, I'm so sorry. I was so caught up in everything I…I totally forgot…"

She furrowed her brow and opened her mouth to speak, but nothing came out. It must have hit her, too. She closed her eyes and didn't say a thing.

I swallowed and prayed she'd say yes to this question: "Are you on the pill, Liza?"

She opened her eyes and they filled with tears as she shook her head. As a tear traced down her cheek, I kissed it away.

"Don't worry baby. I promise you it will all be okay."

She sniffled and shook her head. "Walker…what if?"

Capturing her lips with mine, I kissed her. She ran her fingers through my hair and kissed me harder. I had to admit my heart burst with the idea of having a child with Liza someday. I moved inside her as my dick came to life again. Liza moaned softly as I pulled out and pushed back in. Our kisses were gentle and sweet, but I longed for more passion. For now, though, I knew she needed sweet and slow. As I moved in and out I realized why earlier had felt so amazing. I'd never had sex without a condom before.

"Walker. We…need…condom," Liza panted.

I pulled out and quickly kissed her on the nose before running over to grab my wallet from to the table—my father had always told me to keep a condom in my wallet. I made my way back to the bed, ripping open the condom. I slipped it on and watched the love of my life as I pushed myself back into her, eliciting a long, soft moan from her lips.

I rolled over, pulled Liza on top, and watched her ride me to another orgasm. She held her breasts and called out my name as she came—it was nearly my undoing. I flipped her over and pumped in and out of her.

"Walker, I love you so much." Liza said moving her hands up and down my body.

I bit her lip and sucked it into my mouth, moaning. "I love you too, baby."

She arched her back and cried out my name as I came hard and fast. I leaned over her, trying to catch my breath as she traced her fingers lazily up and down my back. I pulled out, took the condom off, and threw it in the trash. One quick clean up and I crawled back into bed and pulled her close. She fit perfectly in my arms. Miranda Lambert's "Holding On To You" played in the background as we both drifted off to sleep.

Walking up to the track, Layton and my father waited for me, staring. My father smiled that big ol' smile of his. Layton gave me an odd look.

"Y'all called?"

My father slapped me on the back and laughed as Layton gave my dad a dirty look.

Layton came closer to me, his smile slowly fading away. "I'm going to pretend that I didn't see my daughter break up with a guy last night, only to head somewhere in the ranch Jeep last night. Somewhere I'm pretty sure you were."

I swallowed, peeking over to my father. Layton cleared his throat. I looked into his eyes.

"I'm also going to pretend that she didn't come back home just an hour ago with a glow on her face like I've never seen."

I instinctively took a step back as my father laughed. I removed my baseball cap and ran my hand through my hair and was about to plead my case when Layton put his hand on my shoulder.

"Don't break her heart, or I'll break your legs."

I nodded, put my hat on, and forced the words out: "Y—yes sir. I'd never hurt her."

Layton smiled and slapped my back much harder than normal.

He turned and pointed to Love Story, one of the new horses we'd brought back from Kentucky this summer. "Get up on him," he said with a shit-eating grin. "You know how to pick 'em. But do you know how to ride 'em? Big difference, riding a racehorse."

"Hell yes, sir, I do."

I walked over to Jerry. He was the trainer my father and Layton had been working with over the last ten years.

"He's feisty son," Jerry said. "Don't push him. You don't need to prove anything. Your daddy and Layton both know it's in your blood, boy."

I nodded at Jerry. "I got it. Feisty, don't push." I jumped up onto Love Story.

Jerry held the reins in his hand. "Walker, be careful."

I turned Love Story and made my way onto the track. I could practically feel the horse vibrating with excitement as we made our way around. He was getting edgy, so I pulled him back. We made a few circles to calm him. I looked over at my father and he smiled and nodded. I gave Love Story a small squeeze with my legs and he bolted.

"Holy shit!" I yelled as the horse took off running.

He was indeed a natural on the racetrack. Why they hadn't ever raced this horse was beyond me. As we approached turn two, he picked up his pace. I let him go for a bit until we came to turn three. I pulled back some, but he wouldn't listen. Giving him a bit more force, he almost stopped on a dime, forcing me forward. One foot came out of the stirrup as Love Story reared up. I lost balance and saw exactly what was going to happen. I fell back with one foot in the stirrup, but the horse didn't care. My head hit the ground and I cried out. The last thing I saw was Love Story headed for turn four. Everything went black.

I opened my eyes and all I saw was people moving around me. *Where the hell am I?* It sounded like wind roaring through the mountains. Voices. I heard voices. It was loud. My head throbbed and my back had never hurt so much in my life. I tried to talk, but couldn't. I looked from one person to another. There was a guy and a girl.

The girl glanced down, smiling. She hit the other person and said, "He's awake."

I managed to say the word "loud."

She nodded. "You're on a helicopter. I need you to keep calm sir."

*Helicopter?*

My eyes grew heavy again. As I closed them, all the loud sounds faded away.

*Liza. I love you so much, Liza.*

# Fifteen

## Liza

I pulled up and put Walkers truck in park as I leaned back against the seat. My parents had finally convinced me to leave the hospital. I'd headed to the hotel to shower and get some sleep. But I couldn't sleep. I hadn't slept in three days. I looked down at the ring on my finger as I cried.

"You promised you wouldn't leave again. You promised." I thought back to this morning, when Walker had pushed me away.

*"What are you saying?" Walker asked.*

*The doctor looked down at Walker. "Mr. Moore, you could possibly have damaged your spinal cord. We won't know until the swelling goes down and we've run some tests. I'm just saying I need you to be prepared."*

*Walker turned his head. The doctor talked for a few minutes more before leaving. I went to the side of his bed and reached Walker's his hand.*

*He pulled it away. "Please just leave me alone."*

*I swallowed hard. "It's going to be okay. The sedative they gave you will wear off and you'll be able to move your legs. I feel it in my heart," I reached for his hand again.*

*He turned to me. "I want to be alone. Please leave, Liza."*

*My mouth opened slightly and I shook my head. "No, I'm not leaving you. No, Walker."*

*Walker turned to my father and gave him a pleading look. My father held me in his arms as he walked me out. The entire time I was pleading with Walker and Daddy to let me stay.*

I wiped my tears, opened the door to the truck, and jumped out. I made my way into the hospital and saw Reed coming toward me. I walked right into his arms. I didn't have any tears left. Reed pulled back and held me at arm's length. "The doctors said the swelling should go down within a week, but he was able to move his toes a little bit ago."

"Oh, thank God. That's a good sign right?"

Reed smiled and nodded. But his smile faded when he said, "I think his biggest struggle is going to be mental. All he talked about after you left was the plans that y'all had together. The things you wanted to do. How he wanted to take over the ranch and the idea of not even being able to do one of those killed him."

I nodded. "But he moved his toes! He moved his toes! He's going to be okay. We're going to be okay. Right, Reed? Right?"

Reed pulled me into his arms and whispered, "Yeah, sweetheart. Yeah."

It had been over a week since Walker's accident. The swelling had gone down and the doctors expected him to make a full recovery. They'd be releasing him within the next few days. He just had to do a bit more therapy first. I knocked on the hospital door as I slowly opened it. Walker was standing and saying something to the young nurse who was getting ready to help Walker back into bed since he was returning from rehab.

The slender, blonde nurse looked up and smiled. When Walker saw me his smile faded for a brief second.

"Hey," I said as I walked into the room.

"Hey, Liza."

I chewed my lip as I watched Walker with the nurse. He smiled at her. Something he wasn't doing with me. Walker laughed when she made a joke. He barely spoke to me, let alone laughed. When she took his hand in hers Walker smiled at her again.

"Have a wonderful night, Walker. I'll see you tomorrow evening."

"Unless I get out of here." Walker said.

I pulled out my phone. I sent Courtney a message to tell her I was at the hospital.

As the nurse walked by she smiled. "Good night," she said with a wink.

I smiled back and said, "Good night. Enjoy your evening."

Turning around. I caught Walker staring at me. I smiled, but he looked away.

"Walker, um, can we talk?"

"We've been talking every day, what makes today different?"

I approached his bed. "This," I pointed between us. "What's happening here? You're treating me like a stranger. Like I'm a bother to you."

He stared out the window. "Walker! I deserve to be treated better than this."

He snapped his head back to me. "Exactly, Liza. You deserve someone who can actually do the things he promised you. I'm not that person."

I sucked in a breath. "What? What do you mean?"

His eyes filled with tears as he looked into my eyes. "Our dreams. The dreams we talked about the night before I feel off that stupid horse. What if I can't…What if I'm not able to give you all of that?"

My mouth fell open. "All I want, all I've ever wanted is you. I don't care about that other stuff. I care about you. You're walking. You'll make a full recovery."

He shook his head. "I just need time, Liza. I need time."

"Time for what? Please tell me what's happening here, Walker, because I thought you loved me. I thought you wanted...us."

A sob escaped my throat as he slowly looked into my eyes.

The door to his room opened and his doctor began talking as I wiped my eyes.

"Well, Walker. Looks like you're heading home tomorrow. You'll want to use a cane for a bit until you feel your strength building back up. We've got you all set for outpatient rehab. I still can't believe how lucky you were, son. Those muscles should start feeling better every day with the rehab."

I looked out the window and could see Walker's reflection. He was watching me. He nodded when the doctor said something, then looked at me. I twisted the double-heart ring on my finger, trying to convince myself that he was just confused and scared. That he didn't mean to push me away.

The doctor stayed a few more minutes, then shook Walker's hand.

"I'd say you'll be out of here around one tomorrow afternoon so let your folks now. I'll see you in the morning."

The doctor looked at me as if noticing me for the first time since he'd walked in. He gave me a polite smile before excusing himself and heading out the door.

I took in a shaky breath. I attempted to plaster on a smile for Walker. "I'm glad you're leaving tomorrow," I said.

He nodded. "Yeah, me too. Maybe I'll feel more myself when I get home."

I nodded as Courtney and Reed both came into the room. Everyone started making plans for bringing Walker home.

Courtney smiled at Walker, then me. "Everything will be okay once we get Walker back home," she said.

I gave her a weak smile, as did Walker. If only I believed those words.

I sat on the trucks' tailgate as I watched Walker. He still wasn't acting normal, and he only talked to me when he had to. Most of the time, there was nothing but silence.

Daddy came riding up on a horse and stopped short of Walker. I watched Walker's body language change. He kept stepping away from the horse, almost like he was afraid of it. Jumping off the tailgate, I approached the animal. I smiled and brought the horse closer to me.

My father asked, "When do you think you can ride again?"

Walker's eyes filled with something I'd never seen there before. Fear. He was scared of the horses.

"I'm doing pretty good in rehab. Shouldn't have to go that much longer. Starting to lift weights, so I'm sure I'll be back and helping with the ranch in no time."

Daddy slapped his hand on Walker's shoulder. "Son, I just want you to heal completely. We don't need you going off and hurting yourself. We've got some help, so don't worry. I want you to heal—it's only been three weeks since the accident. You and Liza should take a trip somewhere—maybe to the coast. Spend a few days together."

I looked at my father, shocked. He winked at me and I giggled.

"Nah, I can't leave. Still have a few more rehab sessions, and then I want to get to work on the ranch. It's killing me. I feel useless."

My father's expression changed as he stared at Walker. He cocked his head at me. I could see it in his eyes. He felt sorry for me.

"I'm going to head on back. Want to ride with me, sweetheart?" My father asked.

I shook my head and was about to say no when Walker said, "Go on ahead, Liza. Spend some time with your daddy."

My heart dropped and I balled my fists up tight. "I need to talk to Walker, Daddy."

My father nodded, climbed up on his horse, and took off. I took a few deep breaths and stood a little taller, deciding I would give Walker what he wanted: space.

I turned to him. "I um…I think I'm going to head out of town for a bit."

Walker frowned. He looked like he wanted to say something, but stopped.

"I have a friend from college who's staying at her grandparents' place in Destin, Florida. She's been bugging me to visit. I think I'll take her up on the offer."

"You're leaving?"

My jaw trembled. "Isn't that what you want? Time away from me?"

He shook his head and, again, refrained from speaking.

*Fine. If this is how he wants to do this. This is how we will do this.*

I walked toward his truck and looked over my shoulder. "Do you mind giving me a ride up to the house?"

He ran his hand through that messy hair of his, and I wanted more than anything to run *my* hands through it. "Liza, please don't think…"

I spun around. "Don't you dare try to make this better now. Do you know when the last time you kissed me was? Do you have any idea?"

He nodded. "The morning of the accident."

My jaw dropped. I wasn't sure if it was his remembering that surprised me, or the tears in his eyes.

"You've done a damn good job of pushing me away, Walker. You're getting what you wanted."

I opened the passenger side door and jumped in, slamming the door shut and staring straight ahead as I spun my ring on my finger. Walker got in the truck and headed for my house.

Walker pulled up to my house and parked. I opened the door and started to get out.

"Liza?"

I turned around. "Yeah?"

"I love you."

I gave him a weak smile. "I love you, too, Walker. Call me when you're ready to move on with life."

Shutting the door, I walked up the stairs to our front porch. Somehow I managed not to cry. I pushed the door open, but looked back to see Walker still sitting there, watching me. I lifted my hand and he lifted his. When I shut the door behind me, I leaned against it, sliding down to the floor as I let the sobs take over my body.

I sat on Lindsey's front porch wrapped up in a blanket. All I could do was stare out over the water. I'd been in Florida for almost two weeks. Walker had called a few times, but I'd only talked to him once. He wanted space. I was giving it to him.

Lindsey handed me a cup of hot chocolate. "Did you tell your folks about the job?"

I smiled as I took the mug from her. Llano School District had called to offer me a position as a first grade teacher. I was beyond thrilled. The current teacher was leaving after this semester to stay home with her baby, due in January.

I shook my head. "Nope, not yet. I was going to tell them when I get back home." I continued watching the water.

Lindsey sat down next to me sighed. "You should call him."

I glanced at my phone. "I talked to his mother earlier. She said he's been acting strange. And I know what's wrong—he's afraid to get back on a horse. It's gutting him."

"Shit, I'd be afraid, too, if I woke up to hear that there was a chance I might not walk again. I mean, his whole life is that ranch. Can you imagine, though, your job relying on you doing something almost every day that you were afraid to do?"

I turned to her and nodded. "I don't think he's talked to anyone about it. Courtney, his mom, just said he's avoiding everyone. He's been focusing on building something, but she didn't say what."

Lindsey blew over her coffee mug, peeked at me, and said, "Maybe he needs someone to guide him."

Glancing back out over the water, I whispered, "He pushed me away. He doesn't want my help."

"He loves you more than life itself, Liza. He's afraid of losing everything."

"He could never lose me."

She chuckled. "He's halfway there."

I gave her a look. "What does that mean?"

"You ran away, just like he did," Lindsey said. "The moment things get tough, Liza, you can't just up and leave. You've gotten so damn good at pushing each other away that you don't realize how much you hurt each other in the process. Do you love him?"

I swallowed and wiped a tear that had escaped from my eye. "I love him more than anything."

She smiled. "Then why are you here, when he needs you there?"

I pushed off the blanket and reached for my phone, quickly texting my parents.

**Me**: *I'm heading home today.*
**Dad**: *It's about damn time.*

I smiled when I read my father's reply.

**Mom**: *I'm glad, sweetheart. He needs you, even if he doesn't act like it.*

Why my parents insisted on letting me learn the lessons of life on my own was beyond me. Sometimes I just wanted someone to tell me things. Like, "Stop being an ass and stay here by his side."

I smiled at Lindsey. "I'm going to go get the love of my life back."

She raised her mug and said, "That's my girl. Go pack. I'll take you to the airport."

I practically ran into the house and up the stairs. Fifteen minutes later, I was packed and ready to go.

I boarded the plane and found my seat. When I went to turn off my phone, a text came through.

**Walker**: *I miss you. I'm so sorry I pushed you away.*

My heart beat harder. I twisted the ring around on my finger and chewed on my lip. I just needed to get back home. I needed to be in his arms.

**Me**: *I'm sorry I walked away. I love you, Walker.*
**Walker**: *God, baby, I love you so much. Come back to me.*
**Me**: *I need you so much.*

I took a picture through the window of the plane and hit send.

**Me**: *I'm sitting on the plane right now.*
**Walker**: *I'm headed to the airport now.*

I giggled as I replied.

**Me**: *You're lucky it's a non-stop flight. See you in a few hours.*

I turned off my phone and slipped it into my purse. Placing my fingers on my lips, I imagined Walker kissing them. I couldn't wait to be in his arms again. I would help him through whatever he needed. I would never run from him—or anything—ever again.

# Sixteen

## Walker

I made my way down to the baggage claim. Glancing at the arrivals board, I saw that Liza's flight was coming in. I'd had to call her parents to find out what flight she was on, since neither of us had thought about it when we were texting. I lifted my baseball cap and ran my hand through my hair. I watched the escalator, waiting for her to come down.

I felt a hand on my shoulder and I turned to see Jessica. Before I even had a chance to react, she threw herself into me, wrapping her arms around my neck.

"I've missed you so much, Walker," she said.

I was stunned for a moment before I pulled her arms from around my neck.

"Hey, Jessica." I nudged her back and away from me.

She looked me all over and bit her lip. "I've missed your touch, Walker."

I dropped my hands from her arms and took a step back.

She cocked her head to one side, giggling. "Did I spook you, maybe? Old feelings coming back to the surface again, baby?"

My lips parted slightly and I couldn't believe what I was hearing. Did she really think I missed her? As if I could want her after walking in on her fucking another guy?

I tried to talk, but she came closer. "You look like shit, baby. What you need is a good blow—"

I held up my hands. "Stop. Honestly. First off, I'm completely and utterly in love with Liza. Second, you cheated on me for months. You really think you can just show up and offer sex? That everything will fall back into place? You have problems, Jessica."

Her eyes widened in surprise. She wasn't used to being told "no."

"You're a dick. I knew you loved her as soon as I saw the two of you together last summer. The way you looked at her turned my stomach."

"Your point is?"

"I'm saying that you're walking away from the best thing that ever happened to you."

I shook my head. "No, Jessica. I'm not. I'm walking away from the biggest mistake of my life. The best thing that has ever happened to me will be coming down that escalator at any moment and I can't wait to hold her in my arms."

Jessica gasped and then squared her shoulders at me. She smiled, giving me the finger. "Fuck off, Moore," she said before turning on her heels, grabbing her suitcase, and walking away.

*Ugh. What did I ever see in her?*

I felt Liza before I saw her. The hairs on my body came to attention and her perfume invaded my senses. I turned around and Liza was standing there. The smile plastered on her face told me she'd probably heard all of that. Her eyes looked me over from head to toe, licking her lips. My dick instantly jumped. Finally, our eyes locked.

"Walker," she whispered as tears formed in her eyes.

I walked over to her, took her face in my hands, and slammed my lips to hers. We both moaned as she dropped everything she was carrying and brought her hands to my chest. Our kiss was probably more passionate then it should have been for the Austin airport baggage claim. Someone walked by and whistled. That's when I pulled away and rested my forehead against hers as she moved her hands to my arms and held on. Her breaths were just short of panting. I knew she wanted me as much as I wanted her.

I finally found the words to speak. "I can't wait...we're booking a hotel in Austin."

Liza laughed. She closed her eyes and said, "I'm so sorry."

I shook my head and closed my eyes. We stood with our foreheads pressed against each other. "No, baby. I'm the one who should be sorry. I was a fool for pushing you away. I swear to God I'll never do it again."

"Promise me, Walker. I don't want any more broken promises."

I looked into her eyes. "No more broken promises, baby. No more." I picked up her carry-on suitcase and handed her purse to her. "Let's go. I want to bury myself inside of you and stay there forever."

Her eyes lit up with desire. It was everything I could do to not take her right there in front of everyone. I took her hand and practically dragged her out the door and to the parking garage.

We barely made it to the Omni and into the room before Liza and I started pulling each other's clothes off. Our kisses were hungry. I ran my hands all over her body. I couldn't get enough of her. I couldn't wait to taste her.

I unclasped her bra and let it fall to the floor. My mouth took her nipple and I sucked on it as she tipped her head back. I moved my hand into her panties and slipped two fingers inside her, quickly finding evidence of how much she wanted me. I pushed my thumb against her clit and Liza hissed out, "Finally," as I worked my fingers in and out.

I moaned as I moved my lips up along her chest, making my way to her neck. She pushed off my hat and grabbed my hair with both hands, tugging hard.

"Liza, I want to be a gentleman. But, honestly, I just want to be inside of you."

Her eyes filled with lust as she bit her lip. "Now...do it now, Walker. I need to feel you before I explode."

That was all I needed to hear. I lifted her and slowly pushed my dick inside her as she whispered, "Oh God, yes." I slammed her against the wall and she gasped. I didn't care if there were people in the next room. I needed her so much that I couldn't think straight.

I pulled out and pushed back in as she cried out in pleasure.

"Harder, Walker. I've missed you so much!"

I moved in and out of her as fast and hard as I could.

"Walker!" She screamed out as I pumped into her, pushing in further each time, making her cry out again. "Yes, Walker! Yes!"

I felt my buildup and I couldn't wait to pour myself into her. Then it hit me. I stopped.

"Fuck, Liza. I don't have a condom on."

Her eyes widened, dazed, as she kept moving her body to get the friction I knew she needed. "W—what?" She panted.

I blinked slowly. "We almost forgot again, baby. We get too wrapped up in each other. I need to put a condom on. I'm so sorry, sweetheart I know you were coming, but I was about to explode when I remembered."

She shook her head. "Do you have one? Please tell me you have one!"

I laughed and nodded. "Yep." I slowly pulled out of her and placed her gently on the ground before running over to my pants to get my wallet.

"Liza, you should get on the pill. Being inside you with no barrier feels too good."

She giggled and covered her mouth. "I'll go to the doctor this week."

Rolling the condom on, I made my way back to her. I slipped my fingers inside her and she moaned.

"Walker, I want to come with you inside of me."

I picked her up and didn't give her a second to even think before I pushed back into her. She instantly called out my name. I felt her squeezing around my dick and, as much as I wanted this moment to last, my orgasm hit me. I called out Liza's name and pressed my lips to hers. We stood there as the haze of our lovefest began to fade. When I heard someone knocking on our door, my eyes widened in surprise.

"Shit, you were too loud," I whispered to Liza.

She hit me on shoulder, giggling. "Me? You yelled my name louder while you banged the hell out of me!"

I whispered, "You didn't enjoy it?"

She gave me the sexiest grin I'd ever seen. "Oh, I didn't say that," she whispered.

I was about to say something when the knock came again, louder. I set Liza down and she covered her mouth, trying not to laugh. I ran into the bathroom and wrapped a towel around my waist before heading to the door.

Liza got dressed as she whispered, "What are you doing?"

I turned and winked at her before opening the door. My jaw dropped when I saw Keith standing there. I'd only seen him a few times before, but I'd know him anywhere.

He gave me a once-over with nothing but hate in his eyes. We stared each other down.

Finally, he said, "Could you possibly *not* fuck your slut up against the wall?"

Something in me snapped. I grabbed him and pushed him across the hall, slamming him into the wall. I heard two girls scream—one of them was Liza.

"Walker, please don't do this."

Keith's mouth gaped open as he whispered, "Liza, what are you doing here?"

"Who else did you think would be with Walker?" she asked.

"Apologize to her now," I hissed as I pushed Keith harder into the wall.

"Keith, what's going on?"

I turned to see a scared blonde in tight jeans and an even tighter white top in the hall.

Keith glanced at her before saying, "I'm sorry, Liza. We came to Austin for the weekend and I had no idea I'd run into you. What are you doing here? And why are you letting him fuck you against a damn hotel wall like a cheap..."

I pulled back to punch him when Liza grabbed my arm.

"No! Stop."

I looked over my shoulder at Liza and dropped my grip on Keith, taking a step back.

Liza stared at Keith, confused, her beautiful blues eyes filled with anger.

"Keith, we aren't together anymore. What I'm doing here with my boyfriend is none of your business. Just like it's none of my business what *you're* doing here."

Keith ran his hand through his hair and shook his head. "It's just hard to see you with..." He glanced over to me, giving me a look that should have dropped me to the ground. "With him."

The tall blonde took a step toward Keith, but she stared at me, licking her lips. "I think I'm going to go ask the front desk about switching rooms, Keith. Meet you there?"

Keith nodded. "Sounds good."

Keith looked back at Liza and moved toward her, but she stepped back, into my arms.

He looked down and then back up at her. "Are you happy?"

She slowly nodded her head. "Yes, Keith. I am."

He furrowed his brows, but nodded. "Liza, I see the way you're looking at me. You still feel something. Don't you remember what it felt like to have me inside you?"

*What the fuck?* I started to make my way back to Keith when Liza stepped between us. She turned to me and shook her head before glaring at Keith. "Keith. We're over."

Keith looked at her with a look in his eyes that I couldn't read. He glanced at me, then back to Liza.

"When you finally wake up and realize who you belong with, call me."

Before Liza could even respond back he turned and quickly walked away.

Liza took my hand and pulled me into our room. "That wasn't really how I wanted that to end." She sat down on the sofa. "Ugh, the way that bitch was eye-fucking you was pissing me off."

I realized I still was only wearing a towel. I smiled and looked up at her. "Jealous?"

She chuckled. "Nope, 'cause I know you're mine."

I pulled the towel off and tossed it to the side. I pulled Liza to a standing position and guided her into the bathroom. She pushed her jeans off and pulled her T-shirt over her head. If I'd known she was sans bra and panties, I would have gone insane out there. I took her hands as we stepped into the giant, standing shower. It was clear glass, with elaborate, blue mosaic details. I turned on the water and Liza yelped as cold water ran over us. We both laughed.

I placed my finger under her chin and looked into her sea-blue eyes. "What do you wanna do tonight?"

The smile that spread across her lips lit up my entire body with desire.

"I wanna spend all night with you. We have lost time to make up for."

I instantly knew what we'd do tonight. We were going to make up for three and half lost years.

# Seventeen

## Liza

I felt love blossom in my stomach with the way Walker was looking at me. Cold water poured over us, but nothing could cool our desire or the need I had for him. He opened the soap and grabbed a washcloth, then dropped down and washed my feet. He focused slowly on each leg and I gasped when he moved between my legs. I leaned back against the cold tiles. He knew how exactly to unfold me with his touch.

"Tell me you love me, Liza."

I was panting, attempting to drag in breath after breath. "I…love… you. God, I love you."

He lifted my leg and put it over his shoulder; I grabbed onto his hair, knowing he was about to taste me. I knew I was going to come the moment his lips touched me.

He used his tongue to flick my clit and I moaned. "More. Walker, I need more."

He hummed as he began to work his tongue in and out of my body. When he moaned I bucked my hips into his face. *Oh yeah, this was going to be good.* No guy had ever made me feel this way. My body was on a never-ending orgasm high. I pulsed with want and I *had* to feel him. I began to call out God knows what. I didn't even know what I was saying as he used his magic to take me to heaven.

"Walker...condom...now."

He stood up and frowned. "I don't have another one."

My jaw about dropped to the ground as I shook my head. "But...but ...I need you."

He blinked slowly. "We can't."

"Just pull out! Yes, we can! We can do this if you pull out." I didn't even care that I sounded desperate.

He shook his head and placed his hand on my face. "No, baby. I already made the mistake once."

I glanced down and dropped to my knees. Quickly, I took him into my mouth. I worked up and down his long, thick shaft as he moaned and hissed above me. He ran his hands through my hair, giving it a few tugs. I sucked hard and wrapped my hand tighter around his dick.

"F—fuck...Liza...baby I want...Oh God."

I hummed and immediately felt his release hit the back of my throat. I swallowed all of it as I kept moving my mouth up and down his shaft.

"Mother...fucker...holy...shit," Walker panted as his cum spilled into my mouth. He grabbed my arms and pulled me up. I wiped my mouth and smiled. His chest heaved. If I could have, I would've patted myself on the back. I loved when he came undone.

"You do crazy things to me, Liza. You always have."

That admission brought tears to my eyes. I couldn't say when I first realized that I loved Walker Moore. His blue eyes and messy brown hair had had me since I could remember.

"I've loved you my whole life," I blurted. He smiled and pulled my lips to his. We moaned as our tastes mixed together. I never wanted this night to end.

"Liza?" he whispered against my lips.

My head swirled and I couldn't believe the emotions running through me. My stomach kept dipping like it was the first time a boy had ever touched me. Kissed me.

"Yes?" I whispered back.

"May I take you out on a date tonight?"

My smile spread across my face. "I'd love to go out with you, Walker. What did you have in mind?"

The way he looked at me had my clit throbbing with anticipation.

"Well the first damn thing we're gonna do is stop at Walgreens and buy some damn condoms."

An hour later, Walker was walking me down the path toward the canoe rental. "A canoe ride?" I asked with a smile.

He looked down at me and winked.

As Walker helped me into the canoe, I looked back at the young girl who'd helped us. I couldn't help but giggle as she stared. I couldn't really blame her. Walker was gorgeous. His dark hair was covered by a Texas A&M baseball cap. He must have had a hundred of them. He probably hadn't shaved in three or four days and my stomach was doing all kinds of crazy twists and turns at the thought of feeling his stubble brush against my inner thighs. I squeezed my legs together and looked away.

*He's mine.* I thought, smiling as the reality hit me yet again. I closed my eyes and thanked God that I'd come to my senses with Keith. His parting words bothered me a bit, but I pushed it away. Today was about Walker and me.

I leaned back as Walker rowed us down Barton Creek, making our way to the river.

"We have to have it back in forty minutes," he said. "I paid extra so I could take you out and watch the sunset."

As we approached the river, the sun was beginning to set and the light was reflecting on the water. "It's so beautiful." I said. Walker stopped rowing and let us float. He took my hands in his, pulling my right hand up to kiss it.

"Yes, you are."

"I am what?"

He smiled that panty-melting smile of his and my heart dropped into my stomach.

"So beautiful. You're the most beautiful girl I've ever seen, Liza. I'm so in love you. I don't think I could ever put it in words how in love with you I am."

I felt tears building in my eyes as I crawled across the boat. I had to kiss him. I *needed* to kiss him.

"Um, Liza what are you doing?" Walker asked as he held up his hands.

"I need to be closer to you," I said, attempting to stand so I could sit in his lap. I needed to wrap my legs around him and feel him against me.

"Liza, baby, sit down or the canoe's going to…"

The moment I felt the canoe rocking back and forth, it hit me. Oh, shit. I think I'd forgotten we were in the canoe. "Oh no."

The canoe tipped and I lost my balance. Walker reached out to grab me, but it was too late. I was going in.

I hit the cold river water and screamed. Walker was still sitting in the canoe. He was trying not to laugh, but doing a piss-poor job of it.

"Oh my God!" I yelled. "Help me, Walker!"

Another canoe came by. Its passengers offered to help.

Walker moved our canoe closer to theirs and they helped keep it steady as Walker pulled me back into the boat. I sat up, and that's when he lost it and started laughing. I cocked my head and smirked as I turned to the other couple.

"Thank you so much," I said.

They were at least attempting to hold back their laughter. The girl had dark red hair that was pulled up into a ponytail. The guy had brown hair and was fairly good looking. They nodded and the guy finally busted out laughing.

"Haha. Yep…get all that laughter out guys." I pouted as I waited for the three of them to stop laughing.

I stood outside Walker's truck with my mouth hanging open. "What do you mean I have to strip?" I asked.

Walker licked his lips. "God, I want to take you right against my truck."

I raised an eyebrow. "Well, we do have condoms now."

He laughed, but gave me a serious look. "Seriously, you're not getting in my truck soaking wet. You have to strip."

I put my hands on my hips. "Walker Nickolas Moore. I am *not* stripping out of my clothes in the middle of the Zilker Park parking lot."

He came closer, forcing me to take a few steps back until I was up against his truck. He placed his lips on my neck and slowly traced soft kisses from one side to the other, asking "Do. You. Know. How. Sexy. You. Are. When. You're. Mad?" He asked between each kiss.

I let out a low moan as my body betrayed me. Walker lifted my T-shirt up and over my head and I was lost in his touch.

"Walker..." I whispered.

Before I knew it, he was down on his knees kissing my stomach as he pulled my wet shorts off of my body. I stood in the parking lot in my bra and panties as his eyes wandered up and down my body. He tossed my wet clothes into the back of his truck and then picked me up. When our lips touched, I wished we were back at the hotel, lost in each other while Walker made love to me.

He opened the truck door and gently put me down in the seat. I leaned back, closing my eyes as his hand slipped into my panties. I spread my legs in anticipation of his touch.

He slipped one finger in and moaned. "Fuck. You're so wet, Liza."

I bucked my hips, anxious for more. His face was so close to mine that I could feel his hot breath as he looked into my eyes.

"Walker. People...might...see," I said, trying to keep my thoughts clear. Something about his touch made brain turn to mush. I was completely at his mercy.

"We're parked far enough away from people. Just let me make you come, Liza."

Before I could say anything else, he slipped in another finger and pressed his thumb against my clit. He leaned down and kissed me, capturing my moans. It didn't take long before I was gyrating against his fingers, desperate for more.

Walker pulled his lips away and said, "I feel your pussy tightening on my fingers."

That's when it hit. "Oh God, I'm coming!" I cried as he slammed his lips to mine.

Walker talking to me that way threw me over the edge. I hadn't wanted to come too fast—I was trying like hell to hold it off. But his dirty talk was more than I could handle.

After I finally came down, I opened my eyes, met Walker's gaze and said, "I think this is turning out to be the best date ever."

He smiled and winked as he pulled my seat belt on and kissed the tip of my nose.

# Eighteen

## Walker

Liza walked out of the bathroom dressed in a beautiful blue sundress that hugged her figure in all the right places. I loved her body. She had the perfect amount of curves. I looked down and smiled when I saw her cowboy boots. "You in the mood for dancing?"

She smiled and her eyes lit up. Just like I remembered. Liza loved dancing and I was going to make sure it was one of our stops tonight.

"I'd love to go dancing," she said as she made her way over to me. She wrapped her arms around my neck and stood up on her toes to kiss me.

I kissed her lips as I spoke against them. "Do you know how much I love you, Liza?"

She closed her eyes and whispered, "Yes. Do you know how much I love you?" Her eyes opened and she searched my face.

"Yes," I said, placing my hand on her neck and pulling her closer to me, deepening our kiss.

It didn't take long for us to get lost in each other…again. I wondered how long this phase would last. I didn't want to go back to the ranch and face my fears. I wanted to stay lost in my love with Liza.

She pulled back and said, "I'm starved."

"I can be undressed in thirty seconds," I said, wiggling my eyebrows.

She laughed and hit me on the shoulder. "I'm hungry for food!"

I grabbed her hand and pulled her toward the door, picking up my keys as I passed by the table. "Then food it is, my love."

Liza talked my ear off about her new job as we walked into Lambert's Barbecue. She was so excited about being a teacher; my heart soared for her.

"Would you like to sit in or outside?" the hostess asked.

"Is there a band playing tonight?" I asked.

The hostess gave me a flirtatious once-over. She had a pixie cut with a streak of red running down the side. Her eyes narrowed a bit before she smiled and winked.

"Yep! The Whiskey Boats are playing. I'll find y'all some good seats—near the bar, but kind of tucked in a corner." She turned, motioning for us to follow.

We sat at a corner booth, tucked away just like the hostess said. I took Liza's hand and was about to say something when a perky blonde came over. She gave me a big smile, then straightened up. It wasn't lost on me that she pushed her chest out just a bit.

"Good evening y'all. What can I start you off with?"

I smiled politely before turning to Liza. She had a shocked look on her face—I'm sure it was because our waitress was running her tongue along her teeth, staring at me.

"Baby, have you been here before?" I asked Liza. She shook her head and finally pulled her eyes from the waitress, making a face. I couldn't help but chuckle. I turned back to the waitress and said, "We'll take two Ruby Red Mules, please."

The waitress bit her lip and winked. "A Ruby Red Mule, got it."

"*Two* Ruby Red Mule's," I said, pointing to Liza.

Liza waved her fingers at the waitress.

"Right," the waitress said. "Would you like any appetizers? Maybe some crispy wild boar ribs, or achiote-seared chickpeas?"

Smiling, I said, "How about we start with some spicy deviled eggs?"

She winked at me…again. "I'll get that order in right now." She spun around and headed off toward the bar.

Liza made another face and said, "What the hell kind of barbecue place is this? Wild boar ribs? Seared chickpeas? This has to be a place Jessica liked to come to."

I shook my head. "Nope. My dad and *your* dad actually brought me here about a month back."

Her face contorted a bit and she looked back down at the menu. "*My* dad?"

"Yep. Your dad. He got the half local chicken and said it was really good."

She closed the menu and said, "Then that's what I'm getting because this country girl doesn't even know what half the shit on this menu is."

Liza placed her napkin on her plate and leaned back in the seat. "Oh my gosh, that was so good."

I laughed. "I told you. It may not be the country barbecue you're used to, but it's good."

The band had been playing all through dinner and we'd had to practically shout the whole time. When they took a break, we both sighed in relief.

"Shit. I didn't think we'd be *this* close to the band." I said with a chuckle.

The DJ tapped the mic. "Let's take it back a few years, shall we?"

An old George Straight song played. I stood and took Liza's hand in mine, leading her to the little dance floor. Her smile was so beautiful, and I loved how it made my stomach feel all kinds of weird. I pulled her into my arms.

"You look beautiful tonight," I said, moving my lips close to her ear.

She gripped my shirt and held on tighter. I closed my eyes and held her to me. I could feel her heart beating against mine. We didn't have to say a word as we danced, listening as the song played.

I pulled back and looked at her. Her eyes were glazing over with tears.

"Liza, I want to wake up every morning to your beautiful smile."

Liza smiled and wiped away the single tear rolling down her cheek. She was about to say something when the DJ sped it all up. I spun her around a few times as we both laughed and made our way back to our table. Our flirtatious waitress came up behind me, placing her hand on my lower back. I took a step away from her and just stared.

"Anything else you...need?" she asked, as if Liza wasn't sitting right there.

I slowly took my seat. "I think we'll take the check so I can continue this evening with the woman I love," I said.

The waitress's smiled faded. She whirled around and headed to the bar to get our check. I shook my head and looked at Liza. She was attempting to hide her giggle.

"What?" I asked.

"Is it always like this? Wherever you go, the women all flirt with you? Is this something I should just get used to now or should I look into branding your forehead with *Bitch He's Mine*?"

I gave Liza my sexy grin. I glanced up at an older gentleman who stood by our table.

"Hello, I'm Ted, one of the managers here. How was your dinner?"

Ted looked at Liza and smiled. He completely ignored me. Liza raised her eyebrows as Ted continued to stare.

"Our dinner was amazing and everyone here is very friendly. Is that our check?" I asked, taking the check from Ted's hand.

Ted nodded and winked at Liza. She finally couldn't hold back her laughter any longer. I reached for my wallet as Liza giggled.

Ted smiled and said, "Well, enjoy your evening y'all."

I tossed my money onto the table and took Liza's hand. "Come on," I said. "It's on to the next part of our date."

As we walked out, Liza was making a joke about the hostess saying goodnight to me when I spun her around and pulled her to me. Backing her up against the door, I kissed the hell out of her. It got us a few hollers from guys in the bar, but I didn't care. I wanted everyone to know who I had eyes for.

When I pulled away, I smiled at Liza and took a few steps back. I'd left her breathless and she was trying to regain her composure.

"You don't play fair," she nearly whispered.

I took her hand and pulled her out the door. "No ma'am I don't."

# Nineteen

## Liza

Walker had done a good job of putting me into a daze as we were leaving the restaurant with that surprise kiss. We walked arm in arm down Second Street, making our way to Congress. A cold front had come through; it was beginning to get chilly.

"You know, it was sunny in Florida. I didn't pack for cold weather," I said, snuggling closer to Walker's warm body.

Walker chuckled and said, "We're almost there."

I pulled back and looked up at him. "Almost where?"

"It's a surprise," he said, a devilish smile on his face.

"How in the world did you arrange something when I've been with you all evening?" I asked, snuggling back up to him. He pulled me in and ran his hand up and down my arm. The friction warmed my body instantly.

"I have my ways, Taylor Elizabeth Morris."

I smiled. "You used my full name. Am I in trouble?"

"Do you want to be in trouble?" he asked.

We both stopped walking. When we turned to face each other, I felt my whole body light up with ideas—where was Walker going with this? I'd never really played in the bedroom before.

I started chewing on my lower lip. "What happens if I say 'yes?'"

Walker closed his eyes and then opened them. "I get to live out a fantasy of mine."

My cheeks instantly flushed. I needed to know more. "Fantasy, huh? Who did you have this fantasy about?"

The corner of his mouth twitched into the sexiest damn smile I'd ever seen. I could feel myself getting wetter by the second.

Walker tilted his head and chuckled. "Oh Liza. My fantasies have always been about you and only you."

Sucking in a small breath, I said, "I've been bad. Really...really ...*really* bad."

Walker raised his eyebrows in thought. "That bad, huh?"

Swallowing hard, I blushed, barely getting the words out. "O—oh, you have no idea."

Walker put his arm around me again, pulling me back to him as we began walking again. "Then, Ms. Morris, you'll have to be punished for this bad behavior."

I smiled, my cheeks flushing again. "H—how?" My voice shook just thinking of the things I wanted Walker to do to me.

Walker stopped and pointed straight ahead. I looked up to see a giant Clydesdale and a huge white carriage. I immediately went up to the horse and began loving on him. Walker laughed and shook his head.

The driver jumped down and opened the side door as Walker held out his hand to me.

"My lady," he said, "would you do me the honor of joining me for a carriage ride?"

The driver was a bit older with graying hair tucked behind a Texas Longhorn baseball cap. He was grinning from ear to ear.

I looked back to Walker. "Why, sir, do you think it's proper for a lady like myself to be seen with such a handsome bachelor?"

Walker smirked and rolled his eyes. But then he met my gaze and something changed. I was drawn to him as I placed my hand in his.

"You're in luck, my lady, for I am no longer a bachelor. I am very much taken by your eyes, your touch, and, most importantly, your love."

This boy could make a girl swoon. Walker helped me up into the carriage. He sat next to me and pulled me closer. The driver reached for a giant wool blanket and placed it over us. I pulled it up under my chin. The warmth of our bodies under the blanket took the chill away almost immediately.

The driver jumped up and Walker called, "Could you possibly stop by a Starbucks?"

I giggled as the driver turned and smiled. "Let's see what we can do."

I sat up. "Was that a yes? Oh my gosh! If he does, we are so tipping him big time!"

The horse began to take off onto Congress, making his way up toward the capitol. I smiled, knowing that there was a Starbucks a few blocks up.

Walker pulled my leg up and placed it over his leg. The clattering sound of the horse's hooves hitting the pavement was relaxing.

When Walker slipped his hand up under my dress, I whispered, "What are you doing?"

He replied with a wink and a smile, whispering in my ear, "I'm going to make you come, baby."

"Wh—what?"

He slowly moved his hand up more, leaving a trail of heat as I spread my legs apart and moaned. Walker turned his body and gently kissed me. He slipped his hand down my panties and I bucked my hips involuntarily as he moved his fingers in and out. I pulled my lips away from his and looked at the back of the driver's head.

"Walker...we—"

He rubbed on the spot and I was quickly losing control. I looked around at the cars passing us, people on the streets just walking along like we weren't even there.

The driver called back, "Here you go. Just what a young couple in love needs."

The lights on the carriage lit up and I closed my eyes as Walker snickered but didn't stop his relentless finger-fucking. I grabbed his arm as he continued to work his magic.

"Let it go, baby. Just let it go," Walker said, looking into my eyes.

The light from the carriage reflected in his eyes as I excitedly whispered, "Kiss me!"

Walker pressed his lips to mine as I came hard and fast on his fingers. He absorbed my moans with moans of his own as I felt the carriage come to a stop. Walker pulled his fingers from me and faced forward. I was panting like we'd just had hot and heavy sex. I tried to control my breathing as I looked at Walker. He sat there with a smile on his face.

The driver turned around and asked, "Starbucks run?"

Somehow I pulled my dress down as Walker pushed away the blanket and turned to kiss me on the lips. "Be right back, sweetheart. Just sit here and...relax."

Walker opened the door and jumped out. He asked the driver if he wanted anything, and they both ended up walking into Starbucks as I sat in the beautiful white carriage lit up by sparkling, white lights, trying to get my senses back.

I glanced at the Starbucks window only to find Walker looking out at me, smiling.

"Bastard," I whispered as I smiled and shook my head.

I leaned back against the velvet seat and sighed. *Would life with Walker always be like this? Would his touch always drive me so insane?* His kisses seemed to render me stupid. I placed my fingers against my kiss-swollen lips.

I've never in my life been so happy. Nothing would ever top this night. Giggling, I looked around as the people of Austin just drove right on by, not giving a damn that my boyfriend had just given me the most amazing orgasm ever.

I was fantasizing about what tonight would be like when my phone buzzed. I pulled it out of my purse and saw a text from my mother.

**Mom**: *I don't mean to interrupt and I know you're a grown woman. BUT, are you still with Walker?*
**Me**: *Oh, Mom! I'm having the most amazing night of my life. Walker has taken me canoeing, out to dinner, and now for a carriage ride. I don't think life could get any better.*
**Mom**: *Oh, honey, I'm so happy for you both. Will you be home tomorrow? Your daddy and I miss you.*
**Me**: *We'll be home tomorrow, late morning or early afternoon.*
**Mom**: *Enjoy your evening, sweetheart.*
**Me**: *I will, Mom. I love you and Daddy.*
**Mom**: *We love you, too!*

I heard Walker's laugh and I turned to see both the driver and Walker coming out of Starbucks. Walker hopped into the carriage and smiled as he handed me my drink.

"One hot chocolate for my lady."

I giggled and took it quickly, inhaling the wonderful chocolate smell. "Mmm," I said as I brought it up to my lips and took a sip.

The driver turned around and said, "Shall we continue?"

Walker and I looked each other in the eyes. I knew what I wanted to continue. But, for right now, this felt right.

We both nodded and said, "Yes, let's," at the same time.

I snuggled up into Walker and drank my hot chocolate.

"Thank you for making this such an amazing day, Walker."

Walker lifted my chin with his finger until we were eye-to-eye. "It's not over yet."

My insides had been complete mush since the carriage ride. My mind was spinning with the possibilities of what Walker might do to me when we got back to the hotel room.

As we walked through the lobby of the Omni, I had the strangest feeling we were being watched. The hairs on my neck stood up straight. I looked around quickly before we stepped into the elevator, but I saw nothing.

The elevator doors closed and, as Walker pushed me against the side and kissed me, all my worry melted away. The doors opened and he picked me up. I ran my fingers through his hair as he walked us to our room. Walker held me while he skillfully managed to open the door and carry me into the room. When he slid me down and my feet touched the ground, I felt like the earth was rocking. I closed my eyes and sighed. "Walker, your kisses leave me breathless. I want more every time your lips touch mine."

He lifted his hand and pushed my hair behind my ear. He cupped my face with his hands and searched my face intently. "Liza, I can't even begin to tell you the feelings that your kisses evoke in me. Your touch drives me insane with desire. Your smile makes my stomach feel like I'm on a crazy roller coaster. Your laugh moves through my body and fills it with such amazing warmth I can't put it into words. You're my world, Liza. I'm afraid I'm addicted to these things. I'm going to need you with me all the time."

I swallowed as Walker slowly sank to one knee. My heart dropped and I was brought back to that day in the barn. The day Walker kissed me for the first time and a promise was made.

Walker took my hands in his. He looked up at me, and my breath caught. His stubble had grown longer, and I wanted nothing more than to feel it against my skin. His blue eyes were burning with passion.

"Taylor Elizabeth Morris, will you do me the honor of being mine forever?"

I covered my mouth and dropped to the floor, wrapping my arms around his neck. My lips found his and we got lost in our desire. When we finally pulled back, I smiled as Walker used his thumb to wipe a tear away from my face.

"I feel like all I've done is cried today. I'm an emotional mess," I sobbed.

Walker grinned. "My lady still hasn't given me a firm 'yes.' I realize I have no ring, but an answer would be pretty nice."

I laughed as I nodded. "Yes! A million times over. It was always yes for you."

Walker's eyes surveyed my face before landing on my lips. "Liza, I want to make love to you. Your punishment will have to be another night. Right now I just want to be inside your body."

I bit my lip. Walker pulled my dress up and over my head. We moved slowly this time, taking in every single movement, sound, and look. I pulled Walker's T-shirt off and stared at his amazing broad chest and abs. I just wanted to take my tongue and trace along every muscle. Walker unbuttoned his pants as we both stood up. I kicked my dress to the side and stood before him in a tan lace bra and matching thong. Walker took in my body like he was seeing it for the first time. My stomach fluttered and my pulse raced.

He took my hand and brought me over to the bed, stopping when my legs bumped against it. He set a condom on the side table, then focused on me. Walker unclasped my bra, letting it fall to the ground. He ran his finger between my breasts and down my stomach to the edge of my panties. Walker placed both hands on my hips and slowly lowered his body down, taking my panties with him. I closed my eyes and tried to keep my breathing steady.

"Lay on the bed, Liza, and spread your legs open for me."

I swallowed and moved onto the bed. If I was trying to be graceful, I failed big time. I turned and flopped onto the bed, my chest heaving as Walker pushed his pants off, letting his long, thick shaft spring free. My core clenched in anticipation. Walker crawled onto the bed and began kissing the inside of my thigh.

"Oh…oh…Walker," I mumbled as he moved his lips to my stomach.

One hand moved ahead of his lips and he twisted my nipple. I arched my back and moaned. Walker's lips continued to make their way up as he sucked on my other nipple. I wrapped my legs around him, trying to gain some friction.

When his lips found my neck, I was beyond worked up. I needed to feel him inside of me before I combusted. "Walker, please," I begged, pulling him closer to my body.

"I want to take you all in baby. I promise, it will be worth the wait."

"Oh God," I panted. "How do…you do …this…to…me?"

Walker's lips found mine. He took my hands and pushed them above my head as he teased my entrance with his tip. He kissed me, whispering how much he loved me.

"I love you…I'll love you…forever…Liza…you're mine."

It was relentless and I was about to come. I could feel it building. I'd never had an orgasm with so little touching. His tip was barely pushed in as he whispered against my lips, "You're so wet for me."

"Yes," I panted.

Between gentle kisses, he spoke. "I'm going to… bury myself…deep …inside you."

"Oh God, Walker, I'm going to come! Walker…ahh."

I arched my body and he pushed his dick inside me just enough to throw me into an orgasm. I could feel myself clamping down as the feeling rushed through my body. I called out Walker's name over and over.

I was finally coming back to my senses when I felt Walker reach for the condom. I opened my eyes and watched him slide it down his shaft. He took my hands again and placed them over my head as he pushed into me fast and hard.

We both gasped, then laid still, feeling each other as one. Soon, Walker was moving in and out of me again, in slow, beautiful movements. Our lips found each other and I was lost again in a world that existed for just the two of us.

"Forever, Liza," Walker whispered in my ear.

Wrapping my arms and legs tightly around him I whispered back, "Forever."

# Twenty

## Walker

It had been a week since Liza and I had returned from Austin. We hadn't told either of our parents that I'd asked her to marry me. I wanted to wait until we had a ring on her finger. Plus, I wanted to ask Layton for permission first.

Walking into the barn, I checked out all the horses. My heart beat like crazy and I was instantly sweating. I closed my eyes and prayed that I'd get over this crazy fear of getting on a horse. I'd almost lost it all in one fall. I couldn't stand the thought of not running this ranch. But I also knew that I needed to be able to ride. Pulling out my phone, I thought about texting Jase. He and Ava had both headed back to UT about a month ago. Ava was the only one I'd told about my fear, though I was pretty sure Liza knew as well.

I walked over to Raindrop and ran my hand along her neck. Someone cleared her throat behind me; I turned to see Liza leaning against the barn. She was breathtaking. But something was off. She'd been sick since we got back. She looked nervous. Scared, even.

I started walking to her. Liza was chewing on her lip, so I knew she was either thinking hard about something or nervous. Usually when she was deep in thought she'd stare off in silence.

"Hey," I said as I stopped and kissed her on the lips.

"Hey," she said, barely above a whisper. "Would you go for a ride with me?"

My heart dropped into my stomach. "Um…"

Liza placed her hand on my chest and smiled. "It's okay to be afraid, Walker, I'm afraid too, but we can do this together."

I looked into her eyes as tears built in mine. She slid her hand down and took my hand in hers as she made her way back into the barn. She walked up to Raindrop and looked over her shoulder at me. "Let's ride her bareback, okay?"

Swallowing hard, I nodded and turned for the tack room.

A few minutes later, we were both on Raindrop. I was holding onto the reins as Liza sat in front of me. We walked for the longest time in silence as I got use to the feel of sitting on a horse again. It had been six weeks since my accident, but it felt like it had happened yesterday.

"How does she feel?" Liza asked, resting her head back against my chest.

I smiled and realized how incredible it felt to be on a horse again. Granted, Raindrop was nineteen years old and probably one of the sweetest horses ever.

"It feels better than I thought it would," I said, kissing the top of Liza's head.

"I knew it would fall back into place, Walker. Sometimes, we have to face our greatest fear to realize it wasn't really a fear after all—just a small hole we needed to step around."

Chuckling, I said, "That sounds like something your daddy would say."

"Nope, I just pulled that one out of the air," she said with a giggle.

We walked for a bit more in silence until we came to one of the tanks. It reminded me of the days Liza would come down here, throw a blanket down on the dock, and read.

"Have you been coming down here to read at all?" I asked.

She sighed and shook her head. "Not like I need to. Maybe I'll see if my mom wants to. We use to come down here all the time and read. It's a good place to think."

Something was off with her. She must not be feeling good.

I stopped Raindrop and dropped the reins, allowing her to graze while we sat on her.

"Turn around, Liza, and look at me."

Somehow Liza gracefully turned and faced me, sitting on Raindrop. I placed my hand on the side of her face and moved my thumb across her soft skin.

"Talk to me, Liza. Something's not right. Are you still feeling bad?"

A small smile played across her face as she looked away. Looking back at me, she said, "I turned down the teaching position. I'm going to continue working for Daddy."

I sucked in a breath. "What? Liza, why? This is your dream, baby. Why would you turn it down?"

She pulled her lower lip in and began to abuse the hell out of it. Something was wrong and my heart pounded.

"Liza, please tell me what's wrong."

Slowly peeking up at me she gave me a drop-dead beautiful smile. "Oh, Walker. Nothing is wrong at all. I just have a new dream and I'm a bit…scared about it."

I pulled back some so I could see her better. "A new dream? What in the world would you want to do more than teach?"

A single tear slipped from her eye and slowly moved down her cheek. "Be the mother to your child."

I stared at Liza for a good thirty seconds as her words penetrated my mind. *Be the mother of your child.*

"We're…you're…" I ran my hand through my hair. *Holy shit. Holy…shit.*

She nodded, pulling a pregnancy test from her pocket. "I had an appointment this week to get on birth control. When I didn't start my period, I was worried. Then, with being so sick all week, I was curious. Now I'm just scared," she said.

My eyes widened. "Scared? Baby, why are you scared? This is amazing. This is…this is…" I looked all around and started laughing. "This is the perfect example of how it only takes one time!"

She laughed and threw her arms around me. I pulled her to where she could wrap her legs around me. Raindrop didn't budge as I held Liza in my arms.

"You're pregnant?"

She nodded. "Are you happy, Walker? Honestly?"

I kissed her with as much love as I could. When we pulled away, I whispered against her lips, "I thought our first kiss was amazing. Then the night you said yes to being my wife—that was fanfuckingtastic. But this, Liza? Nothing compares to having a child with the woman I love more than life itself. I'm the happiest man in the world right now."

She smiled and pressed her lips to mine as Raindrop walked over to the water's edge.

I pulled my lips from Liza's and said, "I think we're about to get wet."

She raised her eyebrows. "Oh, I'm already wet."

I had Liza up against a tree and was about to push into her as she hissed through her teeth. "Hard, Walker. Give it to me hard."

I closed my eyes and did just that as I slammed into her. We both let out a gasp before I moaned at the feeling of being inside her with no barriers.

"Liza, you're so warm, baby."

Liza moved her hips to get me to move but I wanted to enjoy this moment.

"Move, Walker. Move!"

I placed my lips on her neck, asking, "What do you want, baby? Tell me, sweet Liza."

"You...I want you to move..." she panted as I slowly pulled my dick almost all the way out before pushing it back into her.

"Do you want me to fuck you, Liza?"

She moaned. "Oh, God, Walker. Yes. Please yes."

I moved faster as Liza held onto my shoulders, moving right along with me. Our bodies were covered in a sheen of sweat—we couldn't get enough of each other.

It didn't take long before we were both calling out each other's names. We slid down and I held Liza in my arms as we sat in silence and watched Raindrop graze.

"For once it's okay that we forgot about the condom," I said.

Liza laughed. "I'll never forget this day, Walker."

I kissed the top of her head and pulled her closer. "Neither will I. Especially after your dad beats my ass."

She looked up at me as we both busted out laughing. I moved my lips to her lips and kissed her quickly.

"Should we go tell your parents first, or mine?" I asked.

She bit her lip. "Can we keep it our secret for a little while? I want to take it all in. And I think you should probably ask Daddy about marrying me."

I nodded. "Then my lips are sealed until you're ready."

She smiled sweetly and rested her head on my chest. "I love you, Walker."

"I love you, too, baby."

I took a deep breath before I rang the doorbell. I knew Liza, her mom, and my mom were all in Austin today, shopping. It had only been twenty-four hours since I'd found out I was going to be a father. I'd talked to my dad last night about building a house on our property. It took him less than five minutes to figure out what was going on. I laughed as I thought back to our conversation.

*"I want to build a house dad. With the money I have left over from what Mom's parents set aside for college and whatnot, I can pay for the whole thing with cash if I do most of the work."*

*My father turned and looked at me and smiled. "Apple doesn't fall far from the tree."*

*I smiled and nodded. I followed him out the back door as we walked toward my parents' huge garden.*

*My father stopped and turned to me. "What's on your mind son?"*

*"What do you mean?"*

*My father laughed and shook his head. He started walking again, so I followed.*

*"What's on your mind, Walker? I know my son well enough to know when he's holding back something he needs to say."*

*I ran my hands over my face and stopped walking.*

*My father smiled and said, "Liza's pregnant."*

*I rolled my eyes. "Why do you have to do that, Dad? Why do you always know shit?"*

*"Because I've seen that look before, Walker. In my own reflection, just after your mother told me she was pregnant on the night before our wedding."*

*I smiled. "Were you happy?"*

*My father's eyes got watery and he nodded. He cleared his throat. "Oh, yeah. I was very happy, Walker. I can still smell the perfume she was wearing when I think of that moment."*

*"Liza is scared."*

*"I'm sure she is. But things happen for a reason. Would I have liked to see you build that house, get married and live a little first? Yeah. But I just want you to be happy, son."*

*I took a deep breath. "I forgot to mention. I asked Liza to marry me when we were in Austin. And no one is supposed to know either one of these secrets, Dad."*

*My father's jaw dropped. Then he chuckled. "Jesus, you know how to drop the bombs on a person. Is there anything else I need to know?"*

*I pursed my lips and thought for a second. "No. No, I think that covers it."*

The door opened and Layton smiled. "Hey, Walker. What are you doing here? Is everything okay?" Layton reached out his hand as I shook it and walked into the house.

"Yeah, um, yes sir. It's all um, it's all good. Fine and dandy. Yep." I lifted my hands up and said, "All good here."

Layton stared at me as I babbled on like a scared little boy. He turned and headed into the living room as I sighed and rolled my eyes at myself. *Idiot.*

"Have a seat, son." Layton said.

I sat down and looked around nervously. It felt like I was in high school all over again, asking to take a girl out. Except, this time, I was asking to marry that girl and, oh yeah, I'd gotten her pregnant, and she was giving up her dreams for me. I felt sick.

Layton crossed one leg over the other as he smiled at me. He was enjoying this. I could see it on his face.

"So, what's up?"

*What's up? That's how the conversation is going to start?*

I went to speak, but nothing would come out. "Um…"

Layton raised an eyebrow. He shook his head. "Son, if you're trying to ask for permission to marry my daughter, you'd better spit it out. Dallas is about to kick off, and I don't want to miss it."

My mouth gaped open and I sat there frozen. But soon I found my senses—and my balls. "Yes, sir. I'd like permission to marry Liza."

Layton put his leg down and rested his arms on his legs. "Walker Nickolas Moore. I love you like a son. I always have, and I always will. I see how you look at my daughter. I think I saw it before you even knew how you felt. The only thing I ask is that you always put her first."

I nodded.

"You treat her with the respect she deserves and you love her and your kids with your whole heart."

When Layton mentioned kids I almost choked on my own spit. "Yes, sir. Always. Liza means more to me than the air I breathe. I love her so much…it scares me."

Layton's expression softened. "Isn't love amazing?" He asked just above a whisper.

"Yes it is. It really is."

Layton stood and clapped his hands together. "Come on, I have some cold beer and a pizza with our name on it. Let's get our football on."

I smiled, stood up, and walked toward the kitchen. Layton slapped the hell out of my back and started laughing. The rest of the afternoon was spent with us drinking, eating, and yelling at the refs for bad calls.

When Liza and her mom came home, Layton and I were both pretty toasted. It was four football games, three six-packs, and one pizza later.

Liza was beaming as she looked between her father and me. Whitley had her hands on her hips and I couldn't help but chuckle. Liza did the same thing when she was mad.

"Layton Morris. Did you get Walker drunk?" Whitley asked.

Liza came over and sat down next to me. She gave me a questioning look, and I nodded a 'yes.' Her eyes filled with tears and I looked away. Liza was so emotional—at least now I knew it was because of the pregnancy. I glanced up at Whitley who had a goofy look on her face as she smiled at me. I smiled back. Whitley turned and left the room. I glanced back to Liza and gave her a look. I whispered, "Does your mom know about the baby?"

She instantly blushed and nodded. "She knew! It was weird!"

We both laughed as I pulled her down next to me. "Shit, I'm drunk."

"You're not driving home, son. You can stay in Jase's room." Layton said as Liza squeezed my hand. *Oh, hell. I know what she was thinking.*

An hour later and Liza was helping me up the stairs. I was drunker than I'd thought and Layton was standing at the bottom of the stairs laughing at me.

"Lightweight!"

I fell onto Jase's bed and moaned as Liza crawled on top of me and started grinding against me. I opened my eyes to see her grabbing her breasts over her top.

I shook my head. "Nope, not happening in your parent's house."

She stopped moving and looked at me. "What?"

I pushed her off and rolled over. The last thing I heard was Liza saying, "Walker Nickolas Moore. I'm *so* getting you back for this."

# Twenty-One

## Liza

I leaned against the kitchen counter and watched my mother. She was so beautiful. Her brown hair was piled on top of her head and she was humming a song. I thought back to the other day. We'd been shopping in Austin when she pulled me aside.

"*Taylor Elizabeth Morris. Are you pregnant?*"

*My jaw dropped. I looked everywhere but at her. "What? I mean, why would you ask me that, Mom?"*

*She placed a finger on my chin, forcing me to look at her. Her eyes widened in and she gasped. "Oh my goodness. Liza."*

*My eyes filled with tears and she pulled me in for a hug. "Mom, I'm so scared."*

*She ran her hand along my back and chuckled. "Oh, darling, no. Don't be scared. This is amazing, darling." She pulled back. "Does Walker know?"*

*I nodded. "He's over the moon, but upset that I won't be teaching this spring."*

*My mother's smile faded briefly. "Well, I guess you'll to be working for your father a little longer than you thought."*

*I giggled. I'd been working for my father since coming home from college, keeping track of all the vet records for the horses and few other items Reed and Daddy thought would be good for me to learn. Jase didn't want anything to do with the business side of the ranch, so I guess that fell to me. I didn't want to admit it to anyone, but I loved it. I loved the idea of seeing my parents every day, and working with Walker.*

*"I really like working for Dad and Reed, mom. More than I thought."*

*She smiled and shook her head. "Have you gone to the doctor yet?"*

*I shook my head. "No, not yet. I was hoping you and Courtney would go with us."*

*She hugged me again, tighter. "Yes, I'd like nothing more."*

My mother cleared her throat. "Liza? Honey, are you listening to me?"

"Yep, sorry. I was lost in thought."

She laughed and said, "Nothing new there."

I sighed and said, "I think Walker bought the ring yesterday."

My mother spun around and gasped. "What makes you say that?"

I pulled out the seat to the kitchen table and saw my mom's Kindle sitting there. "What are you reading?" I asked.

She got a goofy grin on her face. "A book I read years ago. Just felt like revisiting it." She wiped her hands and sat down. "Now, what makes you think he bought the ring?"

I shrugged. "A feeling?"

She raised an eyebrow. "Oh, pregnancy feelings. They're strong. Listen to them, honey."

I giggled. "When should we tell Daddy? Walker said Reed figured it out and I'm pretty sure Court knows too."

My mother looked away. I sucked in a breath. "Mom! You didn't! You told her?"

My mother covered her mouth. "Oh, God, I did. I couldn't help it, Liza! It was too good to hold in, and I had no idea how long you were going to wait to tell everyone."

My father walked into the kitchen. "Tell everyone what?"

My mother and I exchanged a look. My father was the last to know. I couldn't let him stay in the dark.

"Um, Daddy? I have something to tell you."

My mother shimmied in her chair and clapped her hands. I rolled my eyes.

"Well, you see, I've got um…I have to tell you…" *Oh God. How do I tell my father I'm pregnant?*

My mother jumped up and blurted, "Liza's pregnant! She's gonna have a baby."

My father snapped his head over to my mother before staring at me. I was stunned. My mother was the worst secret-keeper ever!

"Mom!" I shouted. She put her hands over her mouth again.

"I'm never telling you a secret ever again! I'm going to make you wait until the baby is born to find out if it is a girl or a boy."

She dropped her hands and laughed. "Is that all you've got?"

"What do you mean is that all I've got?"

My father sat down and I peeked over to him. I couldn't read his face.

"Daddy? Please tell me you're not upset because I'm so incredibly happy about this." The second I saw the tears in his eyes, I took a deep breath. "Daddy?"

"I'm going to be a grandfather?" He asked. A single tear rolled down his face.

I nodded as my mother walked over to him. Daddy held her and she sat in his lap. I loved how affectionate my parents were. They were so in love, and showed it all the time.

Daddy looked into my mother's eyes. They both smiled as my mother whispered, "Our baby is having a baby."

She kissed my father and I looked away as they shared a tender moment. My heart was about to burst. I pulled out my phone and sent Walker a text.

**Me**: *Daddy knows. He's beyond happy. P.S. My mother spilled the beans to your mom.*

Walker texted back immediately.

**Walker**: *Thank God. I've been scared for my life. I knew it!*

I laughed and set my phone down. My father smiled and motioned for me to come over. My mother stood up as I took her place.

"Oh Liza, honey, I'm kind of lost for words. I mean, I thought you wanted to teach."

I wiped my tears away. "I did, too. But life had other plans. I'd like to stay on with you, if that's okay?"

My father hugged me tight. "Oh, Liza. Baby, you just made me the happiest man in the world."

I smiled to myself knowing that the two most important men in my life had spoken the same exact words to me when they found out about the baby.

I pulled up and parked outside the obstetrician's office. Walker was meeting me here for our first appointment. We'd decided that the first appointment should just be Walker and me. We'd had to come to their Austin office, since the office in Fredericksburg was being remodeled. I sat in the car until Walker's truck pulled up. I jumped out of my Toyota 4Runner and made my way over to Walker. I looked behind me. The hairs on my neck stood up again, like someone was watching me. It was the same feeling I'd had that night at the hotel. But I saw no one, so I shook my head and pushed the feelings away.

"Hey beautiful," Walker said as I walked into his arms.

"Hey back at ya, handsome."

Walker kissed me passionately as I wrapped my arms around his neck. We were quickly lost in the kiss. I jumped when my car alarm went off. I turned around, but there was no one near my car.

"Why is my alarm going off?" I asked as Walker took my hand and walked us over to my car. I'd parked close to the wooded area of the parking lot, since the car was a graduation gift from my parents. I was obsessed with not getting door dings.

I pulled my keys out and turned the alarm off. Walker walked around my car and said, "Holy fuck."

"What?" I asked as I made my way to the passenger side of the car. There was a huge dent on the back door. I put my hands up to my mouth. "Oh my gosh! Walker! How could this have happened? I didn't park around anyone."

Walker looked around and into the wooded area. "There must have been someone who tried to park here, hit it, and took off before we saw them."

It looked like someone took a bat to the door. "Or someone whacked it with something and took off into the woods." I said.

Walker looked at me and then back at the woods. "Yeah. Kids, maybe?" Walker said. "Little fuckers. Give me your keys and I'll move it next to my truck."

I handed Walker my keys and he made his way around to the driver's side. I looked back into the woods before getting into my car. I was almost positive that I saw something—or someone—moving away from me.

"Stupid kids," I mumbled under my breath.

Walker and I stared at the monitor as Dr. Monroe searched for our baby. The moment the little peanut-shaped image appeared, I cried. It was the norm for me, these days.

The doctor did something with the computer and took a picture, then began typing the words "your baby" with an arrow pointing to the peanut on the screen.

"He's beautiful," Walker whispered.

A sob escaped my lips. "She is," I whispered back.

The doctor laughed. "Well, she or he looks to be about seven to eight weeks. You gave me a date of conception. Are you sure about that, Liza?"

I smiled and nodded. "Pretty dang sure."

Dr. Monroe pulled something out of his pocket and began sliding the tool around. "May twelfth is your due date. Going by the last day of your period, I'd say we're on target. As long as you're sure about the date of conception, I'm okay with leaving the due date as May twelfth. Of course, as the baby grows, we can get a better idea."

Walker and I exchanged a glance. He quickly wiped a tear away and leaned down to kiss me. "May twelfth," he said against my lips.

I giggled. "May twelfth," I said, as I caressed the side of his face.

I turned back to Dr. Monroe. "How big is she right now?"

He gave me the sweetest smile. "About the size of a lentil bean."

I put my hand up to my mouth as Walker said, "So tiny."

Dr. Monroe smiled and said, "Yes, she is tiny, but very well-protected. I want you to start pre-natal vitamins right away, Liza. No alcohol or smoking."

Walker helped me sit up as I swung my legs around to the side. My heart beat faster.

"Dr. Monroe. Is it going to hurt the baby if I've had alcohol since getting pregnant?" Walker looked at me. He was trying to remember when I'd had something to drink.

"How much did you have and when?" Dr. Monroe asked.

Swallowing hard, I said, "I had a drink in Florida when I was probably about a week pregnant. Then another drink the night we went to Lambert's."

Dr. Monroe took my hands. "Liza, honey you're fine. A couple drinks are okay. Many women don't know they're pregnant right away, sometimes for up to two months. Just follow my directions now, get exercise, eat healthy and relax. Everything is perfect."

Letting out the breath I'd been holding, I looked at Walker. He winked at me and mouthed, "I love you."

Ten minutes later, I was leaning against Walker's truck. "I have a surprise for you," he said. "Unless you have to get back to Llano right away."

"Nope. I told my parents that we were coming in for our first appointment. I know my mom wanted to come, but I told her next time. I wanted this to be just us."

He kissed me on the nose. When he pulled back, his eyes were smoldering. My core clenched tightly. "Follow me in your car," he said.

Tilting my head, I raised an eyebrow up at him. "Where?"

Walker opened up the door to his truck and pulled out a bag. He pulled out a red silk restraint and dangled it in front of me. "To a hotel. It's playtime."

I bit my lip and moaned. The wetness that flooded between my legs was unreal. I wanted to reach into my panties and relieve the pulsing.

I turned on my heels, walked over to my white 4Runner, and got in. My hands shook the entire drive to the hotel. When Walker pulled into the Omni, I smiled. I got out and took the ticket from the valet driver, thanking him. He was a young kid, probably eighteen. When he winked at me and flirted, I couldn't help but giggle.

Walker came over and took my hand in his as we made our way to the front desk.

"Hurry, Walker. I'm so horny that I'd let you take me here in the lobby."

Walker chuckled and walked up to the agent. "We'd like a room, please."

The woman at the desk smiled big. I rolled my eyes. *Here we go again.*

"Hello Mr...?"

"Moore. Walker Moore." Walker said as he gave her his panty-melting smile. I wasn't sure if he knew how he made women melt with his damn smile. It was bad enough that he had amazing blue eyes that sometimes looked grey, dark hair that always had the just-fucked look, and when he didn't shave for a few days and grew his beard out...oh, lord. I was about to orgasm just thinking about him.

The agent's blonde hair was pulled up into a ponytail. She couldn't have been more than five feet tall. When she smiled, her red lipstick fought for attention with her white teeth. "How many rooms will you be needing, and for how many nights, Mr. Moore?"

"One room. One night. We're celebrating," Walker said, excited.

The agent finally looked at me and I smiled. She gave me a quick grin, then looked back at Walker. "Oh? What are you celebrating?"

Walker wrapped his arm around my waist and pulled me closer. The hairs on my neck stood up straight, and I looked over my shoulder, scanning the lobby. I wasn't sure why I couldn't shake the feeling that I was being watched. I peeked at Walker. The smile on his face made me smile back.

"We're having a baby," he said.

I quickly snuck a peek at the agent, who gave me an awkward smile. I smiled bigger and my stomach did a funny flip from just hearing Walker say those words.

"Congratulations to both of you," she said. "Let's see what we can do for the new mom and dad." She typed quickly, then smiled bigger. "Perfect. We have a suite that we reserve for VIP guests. It's open this evening. It's on the top floor with amazing views of Austin. Let me book it. I'll only charge for a regular deluxe room."

I glanced at her nametag and said, "Thank you, Jenifer. That's so sweet of you."

Walker pulled me even closer. The desire blooming in my stomach was growing stronger. Jenifer took Walker's credit card and ran it through the machine. When she handed it back, she winked at me. Oh, this was a change. Apparently I needed a T-shirt that said, "I'm carrying the hottie's baby." Then women would leave him alone.

Jenifer handed over the key card. "Enjoy your evening, Mom and Dad."

My heart soared at hearing those words. I was pretty sure Walker felt the same way, considering the goofy smile on his face.

As we headed to the elevator, I looked around again. The lobby was an expansive atrium with amazing views of the city. It was modern, yet elegant. The feeling of someone watching me vanished—I brushed it off as nerves.

We stepped inside the elevator and Walker swiped the card for the exclusive floor that our suite was on. He peeked at me and I bit my lip as I looked at the older couple riding up with us in the elevator.

The man checked out what floor we were going to. He gave me and Walker a once-over, then asked Walker, "Are you a country singer or something?"

Without missing a beat, Walker said, "Yes, sir. I sing country."

My jaw dropped and I was about to say something when the older lady gasped.

"I thought you looked familiar."

I jerked my head back. Walker stood there with a smile on his face. Before I knew it, the woman had pulled out a piece of paper and a pen and shoved it into Walker's hand.

He looked at her and said, "You want me to sign this?"

She nodded. "Oh, wait until I tell the ladies about this at our next Bridge night."

Walker smiled and winked her. She blushed. *What the hell?*

Walker signed the paper and handed it back as the elevator came to a stop.

She let out a little squeal. "Walker Moore. Oh, how exciting!"

The older gentleman placed his hand on the small of the woman's back and guided her out of the elevator. "Thank you for making my wife's night."

The elevator doors closed and I turned to Walker. He pulled me to him and said, "You didn't know a famous singer was fixin' to rock your world tonight, did you?"

I laughed and pushed his chest. "That was terrible, Walker Nickolas Moore. Your parents would smack you upside the head if they knew you just did that."

Walker threw his head back and laughed. "Nah, Dad would high five my ass right now, and you know it."

He leaned down and picked me up as the elevator doors opened into a small hallway. Walker walked up to the door and placed the key card in front of it. He pushed it open and we walked into a massive room.

We both whispered, "Holy shit."

Walker slid me down and placed me on the tile floor. Looking around, there was nothing but windows. The view over Austin was amazing. I walked around the room. It had a contemporary Texas décor. The dark wood and white crown molding added to the elegant feel. There was a flat screen against the wall that separated the living room from the bedroom. I went into the bathroom and gasped. It was the most luxurious bathroom I'd ever seen. The granite vanity was huge, and it included a lighted makeup area. When I saw the oversized, walk-in shower, I pictured Walker taking me up against the tile wall. One more slight turn had me staring at the biggest soaking tub I'd ever seen. You could fit at least four people in it and *still* have extra room.

I walked into the bedroom. Walker was still standing at the windows, naming all the places he could see from where he stood. I smiled when I saw the giant, king-size bed. When I pulled back the beige comforter, the silk sheets made me moan.

"You can see everything from up here!" Walker called out.

Giggling, I rolled my eyes. I stripped out of my clothes and put them on a chair that was tucked away in the corner of the room. Pulling my hair out of my ponytail, I let it fall over my shoulders. I placed my hands on my stomach and whispered, "Okay baby girl, you've been good and not made mommy sick all day. Keep it going, okay?"

Walking into the living room, I saw Walker still peering out the window. I leaned against the doorjamb and cleared my throat.

When Walker turned around, his mouth dropped open and his eyes roamed over my body. He swallowed and whispered, "My God...you're so beautiful."

I peeked over at the bag Walker had carried up with us and blushed. I asked, "Are you going to show me what's in the bag or do I have to beg?"

# Twenty-Two

## Walker

My heart had never beat so fast in my life as I looked at Liza standing before me naked. Her carrying our child made her already beautiful body even more beautiful. I wanted to be buried so deep inside her that she'd feel me for the next few days.

I looked inside the bag. The handcuffs were right on top, but what caught my eye was the blue velvet jewelry box. I smiled and turned my back to Liza as I pulled the handcuffs out along with the box. I pushed the box into my pocket and turned around, holding handcuffs. When Liza licked her lips, my dick jumped. When she'd hinted to wanting to play more in the bedroom, I'd known exactly what I wanted to do. Tonight was going to be a learning experience for both of us.

Liza's eyes were filled with desire as I started to make my way closer to her. She bit her lip so hard I could see it turning white. Stopping right in front of her, I reached up and pulled her lip from her teeth.

"The only person who is going to bite that lip tonight is me," I said.

Liza closed her eyes and moaned. I placed my hand on her cheek and pulled her closer to me, bringing her lips to mine. The moment our lips touched, our bodies ignited, and our kiss quickly turned passionate. We couldn't get enough of each other. Our tongues danced in circles as we let out one moan after another.

I whispered against her lips, "I'm going to make you come so hard you'll be screaming my name."

Her chest was already heaving from our kiss. She was practically panting. "Yes, please," she whispered back as she licked her lips.

I took a step back and took off my T-shirt, slipping it over her head. She gave me a confused look. I laughed and said, "I can't concentrate with you naked.

My T-shirt fell to the middle of her thighs—it had to be the hottest damn thing I'd ever seen. I took her hand, leading her onto the balcony. The view of the Colorado River was breathtaking. Liza's hair caught the wind and her eyes were even bluer against the sky.

Liza gasped. "Oh wow, it's so beautiful up here. Look at the river. It's amazing."

I'd set the handcuffs on the coffee table on the way out here. Reaching into my pocket, I pulled out the blue box. I got down on one knee and opened the box.

"Wh—what are you doing?" she asked as her eyes filled with tears. She placed one had on her stomach and the other over her mouth.

Swallowing hard, I started to speak. As soon as my mouth opened I completely forgot everything I was going to say. I shut my mouth and closed my eyes. *Shit. Shit. Shit.* I'd had this whole thing planned out.

Opening my eyes, I looked up at her. "Liza, I had this whole speech planned to tell you how much I love you and how I can't wait to be your husband. I was going to tell you how much I'm looking forward to being a father, and watching your stomach grow bigger. I wanted to tell you I can't wait to watch our children grow up. To sit on the porch and watch the sunsets together every night for the rest of our lives. But my mind has gone blank."

She giggled and wiped her tears away. "Walker, you just said it all."

I made a face and laughed. "Yeah, I guess I did. I wanted to make this special for you, but all I really want…is you, Liza. I know I've already asked you once. But, will you do me the honor of becoming my wife?"

A sob escaped Liza's lips and she nodded her head quickly. I took the ring out of the box and slipped it onto her finger.

Liza was about to say something when she stopped. She shook her head. "Oh God. Oh...oh...not now, baby girl." She pulled her hand from mine and covered her mouth.

"Baby, what's wrong?"

She began pushing me away but I grabbed onto her. "Liza, what's wrong."

"I need...to..."

She tried to push past me, but I brought her in my arms. She looked pale. "You're scaring me, Liza. What's wrong?"

"Walker, please, let me go I need..."

Her eyes filled with tears. *Oh God. Is she regretting saying "yes" to me?* I let go of her as she slid the door open and ran into the room. I followed her as she dashed into the bathroom. I grabbed her before she got in there and spun her around. I was just about to beg her to tell me what was wrong when she threw up all over me.

I jumped back and looked down to see puke covering my chest.

"Oh my gosh, oh Walker. I'm so..."

She quickly ran to the toilet and threw up again. I tried not to think about the vomit all over me as I made my way to her. She threw up again and the sight of it made me gag. I turned around and looked down at the puke on my chest. I gaged again and turned around.

"Liza, move, baby. I have to throw up!"

She looked up at and gave me a dirty look. I covered my mouth when I saw she had puke dripping on her mouth. I looked around and ran to the bathtub. Liza and I were both throwing up now. I turned on the tap, splashing water on my chest to rinse off the puke. Every time I thought I was done, Liza would throw up again, making me start all over again.

She finally leaned back and crawled over to the wall where she took deep breaths. I somehow managed to get my soaking wet jeans off and grabbed a washcloth. I ran it under hot water and handed it to her.

She smiled at me. "I'm so sorry I threw up on you. I ruined our perfect moment."

I sat down on the cold, tile floor and chuckled. "I don't think it's ruined. Imagine the story you'll have for our kids when they ask about when Daddy asked you to marry him."

She laughed, but then put her hand on her stomach. "Walker, I'm not feeling well. Can we shower and just lay down for a bit?"

Standing, I pushed off my boxer briefs and reached down for her. I walked her over to the shower, reached in and turned it on to hot. I led her into the shower and began washing her body.

"So relaxing," she mumbled.

I popped open the little shampoo. I washed and conditioned her hair as she let out moan after moan. I liked taking care of her, and I couldn't wait to do it for the rest of our lives. Holding the removable showerhead, I rinsed her body and then her hair. I replaced the showerhead and turned off the water. Reaching out, I grabbed two towels. We both laughed when I failed miserably at wrapping her hair. She ended up doing it herself.

I took her hand and led her out of the shower. I dried her off and wrapped her in the towel before I grabbed a towel and dried myself off.

When I picked her up, she rested her head on my chest.

"I don't feel so well," she mumbled.

I walked out of the bathroom and into the bedroom. I pulled back the comforter and the silk sheets before setting Liza down. I pulled the towel off of her head and gently dried her hair some so she wouldn't have to lie on soaking wet hair. When it got at least a little less wet, I lifted Liza's legs and had her lie down.

I leaned down and kissed the tip of her nose. "Get some sleep, baby."

She reached out and grabbed my arm. "Please hold me, Walker."

I walked around the bed, discarded my towel, and crawled under the covers. I pulled Liza into me and held her as her breathing began to slow. When her body completely relaxed, I knew she was asleep. I smiled knowing that soon I'd be holding her like this every single night.

I hadn't told Liza that I'd talked to our parents about building a house. Originally, I was going to build it on the back half of my parents' property, but Layton and my dad said they had a better idea. They'd recently bought Mimi and Frank's property. They were the older couple that had land next to Layton's. Layton and my father were planning to split up the property and give Ava, Liza, Jase, and me equal shares. Since Liza and I were getting married, we'd own half the land. I couldn't wait to tell Liza. I'd already gone with my father and Layton to walk the property line. They'd surveyed it and it was now four separate properties. Liza and mine's butted up next to each other. The way they'd divided it out, we all had a piece of the Llano River running through our land. Liza was going to be over the moon—she currently thought we'd be living in the foreman's house.

I closed my eyes and drew house plans in my head as I drifted into peaceful slumber.

I felt Liza's breath on my neck before I heard her whisper my name. I opened my eyes and found the most intense blue eyes staring back at me.

"Good morning," she whispered as she kissed my lips.

I brought her in closer and held her, smiling. "Did we sleep all afternoon and night?"

She giggled and nodded.

"Well then, good morning, baby. How are you feeling?"

She pouted and said, "Okay. I'm not sure what happened. I'm so sorry."

I rose and gently kissed her lips, then said, "As much as I wanted to play with those handcuffs, I was honestly exhausted."

"Me, too. It felt amazing to sleep for so long. I'm so hungry, but I'm afraid to eat anything." She slowly sat up. I sat up with her and held her as she snuggled into my chest. "I want to wake up every day like this, Walker. I don't want to be apart."

"Your dad offered to let us stay in the foreman's house. We can move in anytime."

Liza sighed. "Yeah. But maybe we should look for a little house in Llano. We can rent it for a while. Get out on our own. I mean, we're going to be getting married, and we'll have the baby. I'd like to have a place for her, and I can't picture the foreman's house as the place I want to bring my baby home to." She turned and looked at me. "With our combined incomes, I think we could afford a little place."

I smiled and kissed the top of her head. "My parents still own the house that was your mom's. I could talk to them about renting it. I know no one is living there right now."

"Really, Walker?" Liza said with a smile. "It would be amazing to have our own place to call home."

I laughed and nodded. "I'll call my parents right after I order you something to eat."

Liza pushed the covers away and I took in her beautiful body.

"No, I'll call the hotel restaurant and you call your parents!"

She walked into the bathroom and came out wrapped in one of their complementary robes. "I'll use the hotel phone out here."

I noticed she had her hand on her stomach as she left the bedroom. I guessed her stomach probably still didn't feel right.

I looked around for my phone. *Shit.* It had been in my jeans pocket. I got up and walked into the bathroom. Yuck. I saw my jeans on the floor and picked them up, praying my phone was safe in my back pocket. When I found it, I noticed that I had two missed calls and one text. I breathed a sigh of relief.

I called our home number. No one usually answered, but I hoped my mother would.

"Hello, you've reached the Moore family. Please leave—"

I hung up and then called my father's cell. It rang once.

"Where the hell have you been?"

"Good morning to you too, Dad," I said with a chuckle.

I heard my father say my name and my mother yelled something in the background.

"No call, no text, no hey our baby looked adorable. Nothing."

I closed my eyes. I'd been so excited to get Liza to the hotel that I'd forgotten to call home. "Shit, Dad. I'm so sorry. We were on such a high. We got to the hotel and I asked Liza to marry me the proper way, with a ring. She threw up on me and we fell asleep."

Silence.

"Dad? Are you still there?"

"Did you say Liza threw up on you?" my mother asked.

I must have been on speakerphone. I laughed and shook my head. "Yeah, right after I put the ring on her finger. She barfed on my bare chest and then…well, then I threw up."

My parents both started laughing hysterically. I rolled my eyes, waiting for them to get it all out.

"Air…I need air…" my mother said as she laughed uncontrollably.

"Haha, it's not *that* funny," I said.

My father was still laughing as my mother kept repeating, "I'm okay.

I'm okay now."

"Yeah, it is, son. Yeah, it is," my father said as my mother started laughing again.

"Okay, fine. You know what? I'm going to hang up now and I'll talk to y'all later."

"No!" they both shouted. "Tell us about the baby," my mother pleaded.

I laughed and wrapped a robe around my body. "The sonogram was amazing. We got to see the baby and it was just beyond words. Liza swears it's a girl, but I say it's a boy."

"Whatever baby M is, I just hope she or he is healthy."

"Baby M?" I asked.

"Yeah, M for Moore and Morris," my mother said, like I should have known that.

I chuckled and then said, "Hey, Mom and Dad, Liza and I were talking. She'd really like to rent a place in Llano. Something to call our own." I lowered my voice, "She has no idea about the house or the land. I wasn't sure if Layton and Whitley wanted to tell her. I'd like to bring her out and tell her about the house while we're standing on our own dirt."

"I agree with both of those ideas. I'm pretty sure Layton wants to tell her and Jase about the land. I think it will be more meaningful if you tell her about the house on your own property."

"Our place is available, Walker. It's a darling house and holds many wonderful memories. We'd love to have that be your first home together. Of course, your father and I wouldn't charge you rent."

My heart swelled with love for my parents. I knew they wanted to help us however possible. My stomach flipped. "Mom, I love you so much for that. But Liza and I want to be responsible and pay rent. If we're starting a life together, we want to do it right."

I heard a sniffle and I knew my mom was crying. "Walker, I'm not sure how the hell we did it, but we raised you and Ava right. I thank God every day for you two. Let us at least reduce the rent. We don't want to see you struggle as you start your new life. How about seven hundred a month?"

I knew that was way below market value, but I wasn't going to argue. The more we saved, the better we could build our own house. "Deal."

My mother clapped her hands and said, "Perfect. Well, it's fully furnished, so that takes a load off, big time. All we need to do is get the baby's room fixed up."

I could picture my parents now. My father was probably leaning against the kitchen counter with his dark hair a mess, as usual. I was betting he'd already been out to the garden and picked what needed to be picked. My mother was probably cuddled up against him, with his arm somewhere on her body, holding her close. Her blonde hair was most likely tied up and I imagined her in her running clothes. My mom hardly ever missed her morning run.

I glanced up and saw Liza coming into the bedroom. She gave me a thumbs up. I nodded and put my finger up, asking for a minute.

"I'm sure Liza is just as excited about that, Mom. I'll let her know the good news and we can talk more when we get home later this afternoon."

"Okay, darling. Y'all be careful. We love you," my mother said.

"Talk to you soon, Walker. Love you," my father said as his voice got closer sounding. He must have taken me off speakerphone.

"Bye, Dad. Love y'all, too." I hit End and smiled at Liza. "How are you feeling?"

She scrunched up her nose. "Queasy, still. I just can't seem to shake it. Maybe I'll feel better once I eat something."

She walked over and into my arms. I held her and took a deep breath. She smelled like vanilla. She always had. I told my mom about it once. She said it was because Liza was so sweet.

Pulling back I asked, "Did you order coffee with breakfast?"

"Shit. Sorry. I always forget."

Laughing, I kissed her lips before walking out into the suite's living room. Liza didn't drink coffee, but I was addicted to the stuff. I headed into the kitchen area that was set off to the side of the living room and began making some coffee. They had a Keurig machine—I'd get instant coffee. I fist pumped when I saw the Starbucks morning coffee blend.

I looked back into the living room and saw Liza at the door. She bent over and picked up a piece of paper and a small envelope. "Here's the copy of the bill," she said as she set it down on the coffee table. But then she gave me a funny look. "This is addressed to me. Who knows we're here other than our parents?"

I shrugged. "What does it say?"

Liza sat down and opened the envelope. She read it and then looked up at me.

"What's wrong?" I asked, as I sat down next to her. She handed me the card.

"Congratulations on your new life," I read.

I turned it over. It wasn't signed by anyone. *Weird.*

"I don't have a good feeling about this, Walker," Liza said as she bit her lip.

"Huh. Maybe it's from Jenifer." I said.

She looked at me funny. "Jenifer? The front desk lady?"

I chuckled. "Yeah, once she found out we were having a baby, she went out of her way to be nice. Maybe she just wanted to send us a card. Who else would it be, babe? No one besides our parents knows you're pregnant."

She slowly nodded. "I guess so. I don't remember telling her my name." Liza hugged herself like she had a chill. "I've just had these feelings lately. Like someone is watching me. I can't shake it. Then with what Keith said that night, and, well…"

I pulled her to me. "Baby, you're letting your imagination run wild. Don't worry. I'm sure this was from Jenifer and she forgot to sign the card. No one else knows we're here or that we're expecting, least of all Keith."

She gave me a weak smile and was about to say something when someone knocked on the door, startling us.

"Jesus, Liza. You've got me on edge now, baby."

She giggled and pulled her legs to her chest as I went to get our breakfast.

We spent the rest of the morning with poor Liza in and out of the bathroom. I felt so bad for her. We ended up checking out around nine-thirty to head back to Llano.

This morning's note popped into my head. I was hoping that Jenifer would have been working this morning so I could ask her and put Liza's mind to rest.

*Congratulations on your new life.*

# Twenty-Three

## Liza

*One Month Later*

S tanding in the middle of the living room I looked around. I couldn't believe Walker and I had our own place. I put my hand on my stomach talked to the baby.

"Welcome to your new home, baby girl. This is where we're going to start our little family."

My phone buzzed and I pulled it out of my back pocket. It was Ava. She was heading home for Thanksgiving break and I couldn't wait to see her. Walker and I had told both her and Jase about the pregnancy over Skype. Ava had cried and Jase was already making plans to teach his nephew how to play football. Then Ava had told Jase that he was crazy because the baby was a girl and she'd be teaching Baby M everything she'd need to know about fashion. Walker and I sat back and let them two of them fight like they always had.

**Ava**: *OMG. Wait until you see the outfit I made for the baby!*
**Me**: *You made it?*
**Ava**: *YES! It's adorable. I have an eye for this shit. I sent a picture to mom. She cried, of course.*

**Me**: *Can't wait to see it. Be careful driving. See you tomorrow.*
**Ava**: *Okay! Love you, sis!*
**Me**: *Love you, too!*

Smiling, I put my phone back into my pocket. I went into the kitchen and took in a deep breath. I was making bacon green bean wraps—one of Walker's favorite things. I'd taken the week off from work to fix up our new house. There wasn't much to do. Hang a few pictures, bring in a few things to make it feel like home. The whole house was furnished, which made it easier to concentrate on buying things for the baby's room.

I leaned against the counter and looked around. I felt good knowing that this was the house my mother had bought when she first moved to Texas. I wondered how many times her and Daddy stood in this very kitchen before she'd moved in with him. My parents' love was amazing. They'd taught Jase and me what true love really was. I closed my eyes as a memory flooded my mind.

*"I love you, Whit. More than anything."*

*My father held my mother in his arms and danced with her in the living room as the Christmas lights bounced off of all the decorations and mirrors. I was sixteen and had come down to get a glass of water. It was Christmas Eve, and my parents must have been up late wrapping gifts. The soft hum of Nate King Cole's "The Christmas Song" filled the room. I sat at the top of the landing and watched. The way my mother looked into my father's eyes made my stomach drop. I wanted a love like this.*

*My father gently kissed my mother on the lips. You could almost feel their love taking over the entire room. I pulled my knees up. My father gazed into my mother's eyes.*

*That was what I wanted. That look right there.*

*My mother had told me a few times about when my parents met. I couldn't imagine my father being rude to my mother or vice versa. They'd had a rocky start. My mother had also been very honest about her previous* boyfriend and how he'd abused her. I was shocked at first when she told me. She was the strongest person I knew.

Her words replayed in my mind. "Sometimes, Liza. It's what breaks us down and makes us feel weak that builds us up and makes us stronger than before."

My father dipped my mother as she giggled. "I love you, too, Layton. So very much."

He took her hand in his and spun her around a few times before pulling her back in. She laid her head on his chest and they danced in silence.

I felt someone behind me and looked up to see Jase smiling as he sat down. "They sure do love each other, don't they?" he whispered.

I nodded my head. "Jase, do you think we'll find someone to love like that?"

"I hope so, Liza. I hope that you never settle for anyone less than you deserve. You need someone like Dad." He turned to watch my mother and father. "A guy who'd look at you with admiration and love like Dad does Mom."

I linked my arm with Jase's. "The same goes for you, Jase," I whispered. "You deserve a girl who knows she's damn lucky to have a guy like you."

He smiled bigger. "I just hope she loves football."

We both giggled. My parents stopped dancing and turned toward the stairs.

Looking at us with a stunned expression my mother asked, "What in the world are you two doing up?"

Jase nudged me and said, "Watching two amazing people share a special moment."

The smile that spread across our parents' faces was one I'd never forget.

My dad laughed and said, "Come on, let's open presents."

My mother spun around. "Layton! It's two in the morning."

Looking back at us, my father winked. "So what? The gangs all here."

Jase and I jumped up and ran down into the living room, flopping to the floor in front of the tree. My mother laughed and started for the kitchen.

*"Well, at least let me make our traditional hot chocolate before everyone digs in."*

*Jase got up and followed her. His arm around her shoulders, he said, "I'll help."*

*The rest of the night was spent drinking hot chocolate, opening gifts, and laughing. Jase and I both say it was our favorite Christmas ever.*

The doorbell rang, pulling me from my memory. I laughed and looked down at my stomach. "We're going to have memories like that, too, little one."

I headed to the door thinking it was probably a delivery from Amazon. I'd ordered some art for the baby's room that was scheduled to arrive today. But when I opened the door, no one was there. When I looked down, I saw a flower box on the porch. I looked up and down the street. No one was walking away or driving off. *That's weird.*

I picked up the box and headed back into the kitchen, where I set it down. When I opened it up, I gasped at the long-stem red roses. I took the card out and read the note:

*What could have been can still be.*

*Open your eyes to the truth...*

My hands shook as I dropped the card. I grabbed my phone and texted Walker.

**Me**: *I got another note. It was with a box of roses.*

Not even a minute later, Walker texted back.

**Walker**: *I'm on my way home.*

Walker and Daddy stood in the kitchen. Walker handed the card to my father.

"There's no way of telling where they came from. No florist, no nothing," I said, pacing back and forth. "It's Keith. It has to be Keith."

My father and Walker exchanged a look.

Frowning, my father said, "Honey, you don't know that it's Keith. I mean, he's in Dallas,"

I shook my head, remembering the night at the Omni and our run-in with Keith.

"No," I said. "That night we ran into him he said to call him when I finally woke up and realized who I belonged with."

Walker frowned. He was surely thinking about to that night as well. He shook his head and ran his hand through his hair. "Liza, I just can't see Keith driving down from Dallas to deliver notes and flowers. It doesn't make any sense. He's hours away, baby. Maybe these got delivered to the wrong house. I mean, your name isn't even on the card."

My father picked up the box and looked it over. "He's right, Liza. They might have been delivered to the wrong person."

I gnawed on my lower lip and I remembered our neighbor Christine talking about how she'd just broke up with her boyfriend of five years. "They…they could belong to Christine. She did mention a recent breakup."

Walker and my father both smiled.

"See, that's probably it, sweetheart. You can't get yourself so worked up over things. Pregnancy hormones are a killer."

I looked into Walker's eyes. His smile wasn't touching his eyes. He felt it, too. Something was off. My gut was telling me something wasn't right.

"I'll take these over to Christine right now. Visit with your dad for a bit, baby."

I nodded and glanced over to my dad. He was looking around the kitchen with a smile on his face. I couldn't help but smile. He was remembering something. Perhaps a stolen moment with mom?

Walker grabbed the roses and the card and headed next door. I looked back at my father. "Are you thinking of a moment with Mom in here, Dad?"

He gave me a funny look and laughed. "The first time I ever stayed in this house was with your mother. She was drunk out of her mind and I brought her home. I wanted to make sure she was okay, so I stayed with her. Before I knew it, morning came, and it hit me—I was falling for her."

I smiled and wrapped my arms around myself. "So romantic," I said.

My father laughed. "You're going to make your own memories in this house, Liza. Please, baby, don't read too much into all of this. It's all just a coincidence."

I nodded and whispered, "Yeah. Probably is."

I pulled up outside of Rudy's barbecue. I jumped out of the car and the smell hit immediately. The aroma of mesquite wood burning filled my nostrils and I softly moaned as my stomach growled. It had been two weeks since Thanksgiving. I was now fourteen weeks pregnant and craving Rudy's brisket like all get-out.

I was meeting Walker in forty-five minutes to get our second ultrasound. We'd get to hear the heartbeat today, and I was giddy with excitement. Plus, the doctor would get an accurate measurement of the baby for age. Even though I knew without a doubt what day we'd conceived: Our first time together—the only time we'd forgotten to use a condom.

I smiled to myself as I placed my hand on my stomach and made my way up the steps to my heavenly barbeque. Rudy's was one of my favorite places. You'd never know when you pulled into the gas station that behind its doors was some of the best barbecue in Texas. But then I ran smack into someone. I was about to apologize when my blood ran cold.

*Keith.*

I swallowed hard and took a step away from him, making him let go of my arms.

"Liza? How are you?"

My heart raced as I tried to avoid eye contact with Keith. Finally, I asked, "What are you doing in Austin? Why are you...why are you here?"

He gave me a funny look. "Um, I'm here with my father. We're working on a project down here and staying for a couple weeks."

Oh, God. I felt sick. Keith came closer. "Liza, honey, you don't look so good."

I held up my hands to stop him. "Don't call me honey," I said.

He made a face. "I'm sorry, it's just an old habit. I didn't mean anything by it."

I swallowed hard and reached for my phone.

"Would you like to have lunch together?"

I snapped my head up. "What?"

"Lunch. I'm guessing that's why you're here. To get your barbecue fix."

My mouth dropped open. *He knows. He knows I'm pregnant.*

"How did you know? How did you find out?" I shouted.

Keith gave me a suspicious look as his eyes ran over my body. "How did I found out what? What the hell are you talking about, Liza? Why are you acting like this?"

I was frozen. I couldn't move or talk. "I'm…I just…I'm having kind of a rough day. So I'd rather be alone. But it was nice seeing you."

I walked past him and didn't look back. In the restaurant, I went right to the counter. My breathing was erratic and my heart pounded loud enough to feel it in my ears.

"Is everything okay, miss?" The young girl behind the counter asked. She had bleach-blonde pigtails and an adorable, tiny nose piercing. She smiled sweetly.

"Yes. I just saw an old boyfriend, that's all."

She frowned and nodded. "I hear ya. You stay here as long as you need to."

I smiled and whispered, "Thank you."

I turned back to watch Keith. He was wearing beige dress pants and a polo shirt. Typical attire for him. He was on the phone with someone and he seemed agitated as he looked back at the door I'd just walked through. Shaking his head he turned and heading out to the parking lot. I turned around and leaned against the counter.

Keith was here. In Austin. My phone buzzed and Keith's name flashed on the screen.

**Keith:** *You seemed upset. If you finally wised up and broke up with Walker, call me Liza. We can go for drinks or something. I miss you.*

I called Walker. It went to voice mail. I took a deep breath and made my way over to the line to order. I would get my brisket sandwich and head to the doctor's office.

*Calm down, Liza. I told myself. Deep breaths. It's all just a coincidence.*

# Twenty-Four

## Walker

I sat in the waiting room of Dr. Monroe's office waiting for Liza. When the door opened and I saw her walk in, I smiled, but it quickly faded. Something was wrong. I jumped up and went over to her.

"What's wrong?"

She handed me her phone and I read a text from Keith. I was confused at first, but then it hit me.

"You saw Keith? Where?"

She swallowed hard. "Rudy's. I walked right into him. He seemed surprised to see me, but I'm not sure."

Liza was hell-bent on believing that Keith was following her. At first, I didn't want to believe her. But when Christine told me that her ex-boyfriend didn't send her those flowers, I started having doubts.

I pulled Liza to me and ran my hand up and down and her back. "Don't worry, baby. I'm going to find out once and for all whether Keith is behind this." She pulled away and looked into my eyes. I reached up and wiped her tears away. "Please don't worry."

She nodded. "I'm trying not to."

I smiled. "Good. 'Cause it's not good for the baby. Or you."

She bit her lip. "I know."

The door opened and a nurse called Liza's name. I took her hand and guided her to the room.

Fifteen minutes later, Liza was smiling and tears were streaming down both of our faces as we listened to our baby's heartbeat.

"Nice and strong at one hundred fifty-five beats per minute." Dr. Monroe said with a smile.

The gel-covered wand moved on Liza's stomach. Dr. Monroe clicked here and there.

"By the measurements, we are right were we should be. The baby looks to be about fourteen to fifteen weeks."

The sound of the heartbeat reminded me of the thundering noise of galloping horses.

Liza let out a small sob and looked up at me. "Sounds like horses galloping."

My heart slammed. I laughed and kissed her. "I was thinking the same exact thing the moment you said that."

She giggled and looked back at the screen. "When can we find out the sex?"

Dr. Monroe clicked once more, then faced us. "We should be able to tell next month. You'll be about eighteen weeks, so if the baby is in the right position, we can tell. Next month we'll do a 3-D ultrasound so you'll really see your baby. How does that sound?"

Liza wiped away her tears as she looked back up to me. I leaned down and gently kissed her. I pulled back as Liza said, "That sounds amazing."

"I need to run some reports for Dad so I'm heading back to the ranch," Liza said. "What about you?"

We stopped in front of her 4Runner. I pushed a piece of her hair back behind her ear.

"My Dad asked me to stop by and pick up the contract for Wild Fire. Looks like he's going to a new owner."

Liza pouted. "I loved that horse. He was a money maker."

I laughed and nodded. "Yeah, well, Dad sold him for six hundred thousand. So I'd say he made some money."

My dad, Layton, and I were all heading to Tennessee to check out a horse Layton was interested in. I didn't really want to leave Liza, but it was going to be a quick, three-day trip. Liza, Whitley, and my mom were planning on painting the baby's room while the guys were gone. Liza kept saying it was going to be a big slumber party.

I took Liza into my arms and kissed her. We quickly got lost in the kiss as she pushed her hands through my hair. We kissed until we both needed air.

Pulling back, I smiled against her lips. "We're having a baby."

She giggled and said, "I know. It seems so unreal."

"Do you think he'll know his dad is a famous country singer?" I asked, wiggling my eyebrows.

Liza slapped my chest. "You are so bad, Mr. Moore," she said, taking a step back.

"I have to get back to work. Dr. Monroe said we can start going to the Fredericksburg office, so I made our next appointment for there."

I let out a sigh of relief. "Thank goodness. Driving to Austin was insane."

She nodded in agreement. One quick peck and she was getting into her 4Runner.

"How are you feeling?" I asked.

She smiled. "Today's a good day."

I put my hand behind her neck and pulled her back to me. I rested my forehead on hers. "You're my everything, Liza."

She smiled and caressed my cheek. "And you're mine. I love you, Walker."

Pulling away so I could look into her blue eyes, I winked at her. "I love you too."

I took a step back as Liza backed out of the parking lot. My heart couldn't feel any more love for that woman. I turned toward my truck, but stopped dead in my tracks when I saw my front-left tire. It was flat. Coming closer, I saw a giant slash across it. I stood up straight, looking around. "Fucking son of a bitch," I mumbled under my breath. I grabbed my phone and called my father, silently thanking God that Liza hadn't seen the tire.

After talking to my father about my concerns, he said he was going to call Layton and fill him in. I changed the flat with the spare and was about to get into my truck when I heard a familiar voice call my name. Turning around I couldn't believe my eyes.

*Jessica.*

She was walking up, dressed to the nines. Her pencil skirt was probably a bit tighter than it needed to be, and I knew her white button-down was *for sure* too tight. She had it damn near unbuttoned, and her tits were spilling out everywhere. Keeping my eyes focused on her face, I forced a smile.

"Hey, how are you Jessica?" I asked.

"Airports and now doctor complexes. I'm here to get my flu shot. What about you?"

Liza and I had started telling people about the baby so I didn't think it would be a problem to tell Jessica. I smiled bigger. What I really wanted to do was stand on the tallest mountain and scream that I was going to be a father.

"Just left a doctor's appointment with Liza."

Jessica looked in my truck. "Where is Liza?" She asked.

"She left. Headed back to Llano. She needed to get back to work."

Jessica's eyes narrowed. "Is everyone okay? I mean, you don't look sick. I hope Liza's all right."

I let a nervous laugh escape my throat. "Liza is feeling...different."

Jessica pursed her lips and looked at me. "Different? How so?"

"We're um...we're expecting a baby."

Her smile faded as her eyes filled with regret. "Really? Y'all are having a baby? So soon? Don't you think you're rushing things, Walker?"

I looked straight into her eyes. "No. I don't. How are you and Mitch doing?"

Her posture straightened a bit as she let out a gruff laugh. "On again. Off again. That's how we like it."

I looked over to the main entrance of the building when I heard the doors open. A nurse came walking out wearing pale blue scrubs. "Oh hey, Jessica," she said. "Forgot my cell in my car. I'll meet you inside."

I nodded at the nurse as Jessica lifted her hand and called out, "Okay."

I glanced back at Jessica. "Well, listen, Jessica, it was great seeing you, but I've gotta run. Some asshole slit my tire and now I'm running late."

Jessica covered her mouth and gasped. "Oh, God, Walker. They slit your tire? Why?"

I looked around. "Probably kids. Liza's car got the shit banged out of it a few weeks back. I'll just be glad to start going to the Fredericksburg office soon. It's closer."

"Oh, I bet. Hey I know this is kind of out there, but if you still wanted those tickets for your mom for the nutcracker, I can get them. It's next weekend."

I blinked slowly and mumbled, "Shit." I'd have loved to take my mom but we were heading to Tennessee. "Damn it, I wish I could. I'm heading out of town for work, so I'll have to pass. But thanks!"

I jumped into my truck as she called out, "Sure. Maybe next year."

I turned and gave her a funny look. One nod of my head and I was pulling off.

"Stop pouting."

I turned to my father. "I'm not pouting."

Layton laughed. "Walker, you're pouting. You have been since you climbed into my truck to head to the airport."

I rolled my eyes, sank into my seat, and looked out the window. My father reached across and hit me on the shoulder.

"It's still hard for me to leave your mother. She's going to be fine. The private investigator I hired reported in before we boarded the plane. Keith is in Dallas. If he makes a move to head toward Llano, he'll be on the phone with us. Stop worrying."

I nodded and turned to look out the window. I hadn't told Liza about my slashed tire. She was already freaked out. With Keith being in Austin that day, the slashed tire, his text, the flowers…shit. All signs were pointing at him, and I could no longer deny that it wasn't a coincidence. My father and Layton agreed with me. We'd hired a P.I. to follow Keith for a bit. If something strange happened, we'd know where Keith was.

I rested my head on the seat and remembered making love to Liza this morning. I could still smell her sweet vanilla scent. Hear her soft moans of pleasure as she called my name. I tried to shake the uneasy feeling in my gut. Sitting up, I grabbed my cell phone and texted Liza.

**Me**: *Getting ready to take off. Have fun with our moms! I love you and the baby!*

I put the phone in my carry-on, I leaned my head back, and closed my eyes. The sooner this trip was over, and I had Liza back in my arms, the better.

# Twenty-Five

## Liza

I stood back, evaluating the room. I smiled at my mother, giggling when I saw she had a splat of paint on her cheek. She winked at me and scrunched up her nose.

"We did good, ladies," Courtney said. "We knocked this out faster than I thought we would."

I nodded. "I'm so glad y'all are here. This has been so much fun!"

My mother took me into her arms. "My baby is having a baby."

I held her tighter as she smiled sweetly. "How about we go cook up something to eat?"

We spent the next few hours making tacos and drinking. Well, my mother and Courtney were drinking wine—I had orange juice and water. I hadn't laughed so hard in a long time. I looked over at my phone. I reached for it and saw Walker's text.

**Walker**: *Getting ready to take off. Have fun with our moms. I love you and the baby!*

I smiled when I read it and placed my hand on my stomach.

"Phone sex?"

I snapped my head up and looked at Courtney. "What?"

She nodded toward my phone. "Phone sex. I've seen that look before. On your mother's face. On more than one occasion."

I snapped my head over to my mother as she shouted, "Hey! That is a lie, Liza."

Courtney laughed. "Really? Do you remember the night you got Layton all hot and bothered talking about your vibrator?"

*Oh my God.*

"Oh you're one to talk. You bought it for me."

*No. No this conversation is not happening right now.*

Courtney laughed, pointing at my mother. "Whit, are you denying that was the best damn gift I ever gave you?"

My mother shook her head. "No, I'm not saying that, Court. I'm saying—"

I covered my ears. "Too much! I have to bleach my ears now. Seriously!"

Mom and Courtney stared at me like I had two heads.

My eyes widened. "I'm popping popcorn. We're all going to snuggle up and watch movies and *not* talk about vibrators.

I spun on my heels and headed to the pantry for the box of popcorn. When it was ready, I poured it into two bowls. My mother and Courtney were now heading upstairs, giggling. I rolled my eyes, but grinned. I loved that they were best friends. Ava and I used to be like that, before we went away for college. I sighed and followed our moms.

Then I remembered I hadn't replied to Walker's text. Setting one of the bowls down, I grabbed my phone.

**Me**: *We love you, too. Going upstairs to watch movies with your mom and mine. It's slumber party time. And I think they're both buzzing pretty hard. They're talking about vibrators.*

**Walker**: *I didn't need to read that. Have fun baby. I'll call later. Heading out for drinks with the pops and my future father-in-law to meet some big-shot trainer.*

**Me**: *Have fun and be careful. Love you!*

**Walker**: *You too baby. I love you, too!*

I shoved my phone in pocket, reached for the bowl, and headed up the stairs. I could hear my mom and Courtney laughing hysterically. This was going to be a long night.

Slamming my hands over my ears I asked, "Who picked this movie?"

My mother grabbed my arm and screamed as Courtney dipped under the covers screaming, "Turn it off! Turn it off!"

I frantically searched for the remote. When I found it, I turned off the TV and threw the remote across the room. "Mom. Why would you pick *Pet Sematary*?"

She shrugged and made a face. "I don't know. I thought it would be kind of fun to watch a scary movie."

Courtney threw a pillow at my mom. "You ass. That scared the piss out of me."

I laughed and reached into the bowl of popcorn. My hand stopped at my mouth when I thought I heard a baby crying.

I looked around. "Do you hear that?"

"The sounds of my heart beating rapidly? Yes. I hear that." Courtney said as she pushed the covers away and stood up. She headed toward the bathroom and stopped. She cocked her head and looked back at us. "Is that a…baby crying?"

My mom got out of bed. "Nonsense. You're both hearing things." She walked up to Courtney and stopped. She leaned forward like she was trying to concentrate.

I heard it again. Both of them turned me. "Do you have baby monitor already, Liza?" Courtney asked.

I slowly shook my head and whispered, "No."

I was about to speak when there was a knock at the door. More like a bang. The baby got louder. We all screamed as my mom and Courtney ran and jumped into the bed.

"What the fuck?" Courtney said as she grabbed onto me.

My heart pounded and I tried to take deep breaths. The crying got louder as the doorbell rang. Turning to my mom, I whispered, "What if someone needs help?"

My mother eyed the bedroom door. "Do y'all keep a loaded gun in the house?"

I reached around my mother and pulled out the side drawer. My mother took the handgun and stood up. "Just in case. Let's all go down."

Courtney let out a nervous laugh and said, "Um, hell no."

The sounds of a baby crying again made me jump.

"Someone might need help." My mother said.

Courtney shook her head. "It's called 911."

The doorbell rang again and there was more pounding at the door. We all screamed.

Signing my mother said, "Oh, this is insane. We're just scared because of the stupid movie."

My mother headed to the hallway, and Courtney and I followed. Walking down the stairs, my mother called, "Coming! One moment while I take the safety off of my gun!"

Courtney whispered, "Nice. If they *are* in trouble do you think they'll stay now?"

We reached the front door and I grabbed onto my mother's arm as she looked out the peephole. "I don't see anyone."

Courtney looked out the window. "There's no one out there.

The sound of a baby crying again made us all jump. My mother took the safety off of the handgun and nudged me back. She began to turn the doorknob.

"Mom, maybe we should…"

Courtney grabbed me and pushed me behind her as my mother opened the door. Standing off to the side, I couldn't see anything. I tried to peer around the door, but Courtney was blocking me. My mother opened the door more and said, "Oh. My. God. Call 911 now, Courtney, and get Liza upstairs."

Courtney peered around the door. "Dear God," she whispered.

I grabbed her arm. "Is it a baby? Is she okay? Mom?" My heart sank. I couldn't imagine why someone would leave a baby on our front porch.

Courtney took me by the shoulders. "Liza, there is no baby. Honey, look at me. I need you to get upstairs and lock your bedroom door until the police get here."

I shook my head. "No, Court. Tell me what's going on. Please!"

My mom had walked outside, holding the gun up. I screamed out for her. "Mom!" I looked back at Courtney and used all my might to push her off of me as I made my way out the door. The moment I stepped past the threshold, I sucked in a breath. Every hair on my body stood up as I looked down.

"Wh—why…who…" I couldn't breathe as I read the words painted in blood red across my porch.

The sound of a baby crying started again and I jumped, screaming. My mother covered a finger with the hem of her shirt as she pushed stop on an old recording device. My eyes darted around.

*Keith. Oh my God. He knows where I live.*

My mother stepped over the painted words and took me by the arm, leading me back inside. I frantically looked all over and cried, "He's out there! Mom, he's still out there!"

"Shh, baby, it's all right. Let's sit down. You need to calm down."

I could hear Courtney on the phone with the police. I started looking for my phone.

"Walker. I need Walker. I have to talk to Walker," I said as I cried.

My mother grabbed my hands. "Liza, I need you to calm down. Take a deep breath."

Courtney shut the front door and went into the living room as she talked to the police.

I tried to focus on my mom. I tried to calm down. But all I could picture was Keith, outside my home. On my porch.

*Walker. I need Walker.*

I sat on the sofa with my legs pulled up, my chin resting on my knees. I sighed as the police officer asked question after question. I grabbed my phone and called Walker again. I'd been trying to call him for an hour. I wiped away the tear that crawled down my face.

I felt a hand on my shoulder and I looked to see Courtney sitting next to me. She handed me a mug filled with hot tea. I sipped it as I listened the officer finishing up with my mother. They both stood and my mother shook his hand.

He turned and looked down at me. "We'll get this guy, Ms. Morris."

I smiled weakly as I nodded my head.

My mother walked the police officer to the door and spoke a bit more. Closing my eyes, I fought back the tears. When I heard my brother Jase's voice, I jumped up and ran to him. He took me in his arms and held me as I finally let the flood of tears go.

"It's okay, pumpkin. I'm here. Shh, I'm here."

"Jase, he was here. He was here *at my house*," I sobbed into his chest.

Jase held me tighter and I instantly felt better.

"Mom, I'm taking y'all to our house tonight. I called a few buddies who are going to come out, too." He lifted my chin. "Go pack a bag, pumpkin. We're going home."

I nodded and started to make my way upstairs. But I stopped and turned around. My mother was already walking behind me. I tried to smile, but failed. She linked her arm with mine as we continued up the stairs. We quickly packed a bag and I jumped when my cell phone rang. I pulled it out of my pocket and cried when I saw Walker's name.

My hands trembled as I barely got his name past my lips.

# Twenty-Six

## Walker

I was shocked listening to Liza try to tell me what had happened. She was crying so hard that Whitley ended up taking the phone and telling me everything. I ran my hand through my hair and fought like hell to keep my emotions at bay.

"Whitley, I'm heading to the airport right now," I said.

I glanced up and saw my father walking up to me while he was on the phone. Layton had called Whitley at the same time I'd called Liza. When Layton had told my father what was going on, he'd jumped on the phone and called the private investigator.

"I know it's late, but I have to try and get home to her, Whitley," I said as I watched my father and Layton. "Please don't let her out of your sight."

My father said something to Layton.

"Mother fucker!" Layton said. "How?"

Whitley's voice faded out as I tried to concentrate on what my father was saying.

"Yeah, um...may I speak to her again?" I asked.

"Walker? I'm so scared. He's still out there." Liza's said, her voice shaky.

"Baby, you're going to be safe. Whitley said Jase is having a bunch of guys come out the ranch. He'll keep you safe until I get there. I'm heading to the airport and getting on the first plane home. I promise, I'll be there as fast as I can."

"O—okay."

Closing my eyes I thanked God that she was okay. "Try to keep calm, baby."

Liza sniffled. "Jase is ready to go. I need you to be here. I need to be in your arms."

My heart broke more with every plea. "I need you to be in my arms, too. I love you, Liza."

"I love you, too, Walker. Be careful."

The line went dead and I turned to Layton and my father.

My father looked stricken. "He lost Keith hours ago."

Anger raced through my blood. "What? How the hell did he lose him?"

"Traffic. He doesn't think Keith knew he was being tailed. They got caught in a traffic jam due to an accident. Somehow Keith was able to navigate through it faster and the P.I. lost him. He's been camped out at Keith's house. He hasn't returned home yet. He's got a friend checking to see if Keith went to the airport."

"We need to get back home," I said. "I'm heading to the airport."

Mr. Robertson got up from where he'd been sitting, taking this all in. "I have a private jet. Let me call and get it ready to go."

Layton walked over to Mr. Robertson and put his hand on his shoulder. "Rich, are you sure? I'll buy the horse. Hell I'll buy three of them for this."

Mr. Robertson's horses were the reason we'd made this trip. He was probably one of the best-known breeders in Tennessee.

He smiled. "Layton, let's just get y'all home. We'll talk business over the phone later this week."

Liza leapt into my arms the moment I walked into the house. There were two of our old buddies from high school at the front gate and another guy at the front door of the house. Until we caught Keith, I wasn't planning to leave Liza's side.

Liza pulled back and frantically kissed all over my face. "Thank God you're home." She said as she finally landed her lips on mine.

I was acutely aware that our parents were right there. I put her down without breaking our kiss. When I pulled back, tears were streaming down her face. I wiped them away with my thumbs.

"I'm here. I'm not going to leave, baby."

She smiled slightly, and I could sense her body relaxing. Layton came over and Liza walked into his arms. He held her for a while before placing his hand on her cheek.

"We'll find him. I swear to you."

Liza nodded. "I know you will, Daddy. I know." Liza turned to me with a weak smile. She had dark circles under her eyes and her face was pale.

My mom must have noticed as well. "Liza, now that Walker's here, why don't you go get some sleep?" She looked around. "I think we could *all* use some sleep."

Whitley nodded. "Reed, Court, take the guest bedroom." Turning to Jase she said, "The guys can go home, Jase. Or they're more than welcome to camp out in the foreman's house."

Jase nodded. "I'll tell them. Since it's late, I'm sure they'll just crash here for a bit."

I took Liza's hand in mine as she said goodnight and gave everyone a kiss on the cheek. We headed upstairs to her bedroom. My parents were staying in the guest room next to Liza's.

Crawling into bed, I pulled Liza close. Her breathing was slowing down, becoming deeper. "I hate him, Walker. I hate him for scaring me like this. Why is he doing this?"

My body was so fatigued. Every muscle felt like it weighed ten times what it should.

I took a shaky breath. I'd do whatever I needed to do to protect Liza and our child. I whispered, "I don't know, Liza. But I swear he won't get near you again. I promise you."

It had been almost two days since the incident happened at our house. The police where done gathering evidence, and they said that whoever did this had covered his or her tracks. Liza was curled up on the sofa next to my mother, both reading a book. I smiled as I watched both of their faces change as they read.

My father tapped me on the shoulder. "Take a walk with me?"

I shook my head. "Nah."

Liza set her book in her lap. "Walker. You've been next to me since you got back from Tennessee. I promise I'll be okay. Your mom is here. Go get some fresh air, baby."

I did need to get out and clear my head. There was still no word on Keith's whereabouts. When the P.I. stopped at Keith's parents', his mom had screamed to leave her son alone and then slammed the door in his face. The police had already been by to question them. Apparently, they were very angry and had accused Liza of slander.

I stood up. "Please don't leave her side mom."

Liza smiled and my mother gave me a wink. "Since my car is in the shop," she said. "I don't think we'll be going anywhere. Go on, honey. Go get some fresh air."

Walking over, I leaned down and brushed my lips against Liza's. I knew that, if I kissed her, I'd want to take her up to my room and make love to her like I had this afternoon when she'd finally woken up. We'd all eaten a late lunch at Layton and Whitley's before coming back here for the night.

I followed my dad out the front door. He needed to grab his work cell from the truck.

"Dad, I'm not so sure about leaving Liza."

Opening the truck door, he grabbed his phone, and put it in his back pocket. "Walker, she's going to be fine. Come on, let's walk."

We started down a path that led to the back of our house, going past the old tree house I couldn't help but smile. So many memories in that damn thing.

I noticed my dad staring at me. "What's on your mind, Dad?"

He laughed and said, "I never could hold anything back from you, Walker."

I chuckled. "No, sir. Just like I can't hold anything back from you."

My father nodded. "Are you doing okay, Walker? How's Liza? She's putting up a damn good front today."

I nodded my head. "Yeah, she's one hell of a strong person. She keeps saying she's fine now that I'm back. But I don't want to take her home, Dad, with Keith still missing. What if he's just watching the house for her to return? I mean, that note he wrote on the front porch—what kind of sick bastard does that?"

My father's phone buzzed with a text message. He pulled out his personal cell and read it. His face turned white as he stopped walking and finally looked at me.

My heart stopped for a second before slamming in my chest. "What? What's wrong?"

His mouth was open slightly, like he was trying to let what he'd read sink in. He shook his head and was about to say something when we heard Liza scream.

"Liza!" We both yelled.

As we ran, I said, "It sounded like she was…"

Then I heard a gunshot. My whole world stopped.

It took everything I had to keep my legs moving. We were almost at the house when I saw someone running away, dressed in a grey hoodie, their face concealed by the hood.

I was torn. Did I go to Liza, or go after this prick and end this now? "Get Liza!" I yelled out to my dad. "I'm going after him!"

I took off running faster. Keith ran into the woods. I ran faster. *Liza. Please be okay.*

*The baby.*

It didn't take long to catch up with the asshole. I grabbed him, knocking him to the ground. I was going to beat the living shit out of him. I grabbed him, pulled him over, and raised my fist.

"No! Walker no!"

It took me a second to register the voice…and then the face.

*Jessica.*

I stuttered as I looked down at her. "Wh—what…are you…"

She attempted to punch me in the stomach, but I grabbed her hands and pushed them over her head. "What have you done? Why, Jessica?"

Her eyes filled with anger as she spat out, "I won't let her have your baby. That's my baby! Mine!"

Bile began to build in the back of my throat. It had been Jessica all along.

*Holy fuck. It was Jessica. Not Keith.*

I kept glancing at Jessica as she sat in the back of the police car. My heart hadn't stopped pounding since I first heard that gunshot. I looked over my shoulder and saw Liza standing with my mother's arms around her. Right after my father and I left for our walk, my mother and Liza had decided to go out to the garden. Liza had screamed when she came upon a rattlesnake. My mother had grabbed her shotgun and shot at the snake.

I closed my eyes, saying a prayer of thanks that they'd gone outside. Jessica told the police she'd overheard my father and I talking as we made our way to his truck. Jessica then watched us walk away. When she could no longer see us, she'd made her way into the house. She hadn't seen my mother's car, and thought Liza would be alone in the house. Jessica had been in the living room about to search the house when she heard the gunshot and ran like hell. That was when we'd seen her coming out of the house and running toward the woods.

One of the Blanco County sheriffs was finishing up with Liza and my mother. He turned and came over to me.

"I don't think you're going to have to worry about her anytime soon. She's confessed to everything. From hitting the vehicle with a bat, to what she'd planned on doing when she found your fiancée in the house alone."

My blood ran cold and every hair on my neck stood up. "What were her plans?"

He kicked the dirt. "She was going to try to make Ms. Morris…loose the baby."

"I just don't understand how she could do this. I just can't grasp this. I was the one who told her I'd be out of town." I rested my face in my hands and sighed.

"You didn't know, son. Don't beat yourself up," the sheriff said. "Ms. Morris is okay. Ms. Burch will not be bothering either of you ever again."

Peeking over to Liza, I nodded. If Jessica ever came near Liza or our child again, I'd kill her. That is promise I didn't intend on breaking.

# Twenty-Seven

## Liza

It had been two months since the incident with Jessica. Finally relaxed, I placed my hand on my baby bump. Walker had started building on the land our parents had given us. I'd been feeling the baby move since I was at about eighteen weeks. Walker had yet to feel her move, and it was killing him.

I smiled as I walked around the house. It was going to be beautiful. When Walker had told me about his plans to build, I'd cried. Then again, I'd been a crying fool this whole pregnancy.

I looked up at the wood beams and inhaled deeply. I loved the smell of fresh-cut wood. My father and Walker's dad, Reed, were both helping with the house. Jase had helped over Christmas break while Ava and I were shopping for maternity clothes. Ava had been thrilled with the stuff we bought. Of course, she'd taken it all back to her parents' for a few days of tweaking at her sewing machine, adding her special touch to each outfit. When I got them back, I felt like I was dressed in a special designer line. Ava was heading to Italy with Jase over the summer. She was interning with a designer she'd been hoping to work for. Jase was pretty jazzed to be heading to Italy as well for the summer.

Walker's voice pulled me out of my thoughts. "Are you liking it?" he asked as he smiled his panty-melting smile. His blue eyes lit up. I knew exactly what I needed.

"I love it, but I know something I'd love more," I said as I licked my lips. I moved closer and put my hand on his chest. Looking into his eyes, I whispered, "I want you to have your way with, me and I don't want it gentle. I want it hard. I want to be tied up."

Walker's eyes filled with desire. "I still have the handcuffs in my truck."

I moaned at the thought. "Yes, please."

Walker turned and headed out of the house. I spun around, taking in everything. *Where the hell where we going to have sex?*

I heard Walker walking back in, carrying the same small bag back from the day he asked me to marry him at the Omni. He also had something huge and black. He walked right by me saying, "Follow me to the master bedroom."

I followed him into what would be our bedroom. It was huge, and I could picture it already. I smiled as I looked over at the bay window. I'd told Walker I wanted bookshelves and a reading nook—he hadn't let me down.

Walker handed me the bag and placed the black raft-looking thing on the floor. My eyes moved up and down his body. He looked hot as hell in old worn out jeans, a light blue T-shirt, an A&M cap and his cowboy boots. I couldn't wait to feel him inside of me.

When he began to unfold the black thing, I saw that it was a blow up mattress. I giggled and rolled my eyes, wondering how long he'd had that in his truck.

Walker used an electric pump to inflate the mattress. He stood and turned to me. "Undress yourself, Liza."

The authority in his voice had my insides melting. I set the bag down and lifted my T-shirt over my head, tossing it to the side. Walker glanced at my belly. His eyes moved up and landed on my chest. He licked his lips. I grinned, knowing what my body did to him. He always made me feel sexy. I unbuttoned my pants and pulled them down, hooking my panties with them as I pushed them off and kicked them to the side. The only thing I still had on was my bra and my not-so-sexy flip-flops. No way was I taking my shoes off on this dirty floor. Walker came over and cupped my breasts, and I sucked in a breath.

"So damn perfect," he said.

In one movement, he had my bra off and soon had my nipples in his mouth. I tipped my head back and moaned at both the pleasure and the pain.

"Walker," I whispered, pushing my hands through his hair, tugging slightly.

He let out a deep moan. "Get on the mattress, Liza. I'm going to taste you."

I moved quickly as I felt the wetness grow between my legs. I lay on my back and got ready for Walker to work his magic. Walker moved in between my legs, pushing them open and exposing even more. I lifted my head and looked at him. He moved his eyes up my body until we were staring at each other.

"I love how wet you are for me, Liza. I can see your pussy glistening with arousal."

My mouth parted slightly at his crudeness, and I felt my insides pulsing. I tipped my head back down and whispered, "Oh, God."

He kissed and sucked all around my clit, making me thrash my head around. "Don't play, Walker," I panted. "Do it!" My voice was laced with need, and I didn't care. I was so worked up that just one touch of his tongue on my clit would make me come.

He tormented me with kisses. He sucked my swollen lips and moaned. I grabbed his head, trying to move him.

"Damn it, Walker. Fuck me with your tongue."

He chuckled and I felt his hot breath. "I like when you talk dirty to me, Liza."

Ugh. I was going to end up getting *myself* off here in another minute. I moved my hand down and touched my clit, making my hips jerk. Walker got up quickly, and in my dazed state of desire and lust, I barely registered what he was doing. I rubbed my clit as I felt my build.

"Yes. Yes," I mumbled. "Oh it feels good." The air mattress moved and Walker grabbed my hand and stopped me, just shy of an orgasm. "Damn it! No!"

I felt cold metal against my wrist. Walker was putting the handcuffs on me.

"Put your hands above your head Liza."

I quickly did what he asked. Walker moved up, pushing my hands together. His hard dick was right in my face, so I licked up the shaft, making it twitch. I smiled and wished I could take him in my mouth. When he clicked the other handcuff on, I tried to move my hands, but they were locked above my head.

"Don't pull hard, baby, Walker said. "You're cuffed around a copper pipe."

I looked up and behind me. When I pulled, the pipe stopped the handcuffs.

"I believe that months ago you said you were bad girl. It's time for your punishment."

Walker moved his dick so that it barely touched my lips. I licked it again, and Walker closed his eyes. He began stroking his long, thick, hard shaft.

*Jesus I need to come.* I was so turned on just watching him touch himself. I licked my lips. He moved his hand slowly at first, then picked up the pace.

"Do you like watching me do this, Liza?"

Nodding, I said, "Yes. I'm so turned on, Walker. Please. Please I need to come."

He kept moving his hand up and down. The sounds his hand made as it glided over his dick was driving me insane. I jerked on the handcuffs and groaned in frustration.

Walker stopped playing with himself as he began sucking my nipple. I cried out as he gently bit it. My mind spun as I felt my build up. He wasn't even touching me.

"Walker. Oh, God. I think I'm going to…"

Walker sat up and the feeling vanished in an instant.

"No!" I cried. I pulled on the cuffs again. I needed to touch myself. "I need to touch you, Walker."

He smiled as he placed soft kisses around my breast. He moved to my stomach and placed his hands on it, kissing it gently.

"Don't you dare talk to her and ruin my moment of desire," I cried out.

Walker chuckled and made his way down. His tongue ran down the inside of my thigh and I about jumped off the blow-up mattress. He was killing me slowly.

"If you don't make me come, no sex for a month!" I yelled attempting to pull my hands free again. The metal pipe clanged in response.

"Is that so, Liza?" He quickly licked my clit and I screamed. Then he blew on it, and I could feel the buildup in my toes.

"So…close…Walker…please," I whispered, shaking my head back and forth.

When he slipped his fingers inside me, I cried out in relief. The movement back and forth felt like heaven.

"Yes, finally." I whimpered

I had never been brought to orgasm so many times only to have it taken away. I knew that the moment my orgasm hit I was going to come hard.

"What do you want, Liza? Do you want me to make you come and then make love to you? Or do you want to be fucked?"

I swallowed hard. My insides were quivering with desire. Walker talking dirty to me only heightened my need. "Fucked," I panted. "I want…to …be…"

Then his mouth attacked my clit. His tongue moved swiftly as his fingers fucked me. When he took his fingers out and moved his tongue, I lost it. My orgasm hit so fast and hard that I screamed incoherently. I could feel my insides pulse over and over while Walker never let up. I'd never had an orgasm last this long. Again, he pushed his fingers in and another wave hit. Soon, I was pretty sure I'd left my body.

My core pulsed as I felt Walker doing something with my hands as they fell free of the handcuffs. He lifted me up and I wrapped my legs around him as I sat on his lap and he held me. I could feel his dick jumping against me. I was breathing like I'd just run a marathon. I loved that we'd just had this moment in our new house. Nothing could make it better. Then the baby began moving like crazy.

"She's moving around…a lot," I panted out.

Walker slowly laid me back down as he moved next to me. My breathing had calmed, but I swore my insides were still pulsing. Walker placed his hand on my stomach and talked to our baby.

"Hey buddy, when are you going to move so I…"

I felt the baby kick. Walker pulled his hand away, then quickly put it back on my belly. *He felt her. He finally felt her.* I giggled as the tears built up in my eyes. The baby moved again, this time stronger. The tear rolling down Walker's cheek made my heart soar.

This moment was now a thousand times better.

Walker kept his hand on my stomach, talking to her as she moved. When she finally settled, he kissed me. His kiss was filled with so much love that I could feel it flowing from his body into mine. He shifted his body and began to make love to me.

These were the moments that I lived for. Walker and I together as one. When he whispered in my ear that he was about to come, I whispered his name back and we both reached heaven together.

# Twenty-Eight

## Walker

I watched as our baby moved all over the place on the screen.

"She sure is active," Dr. Monroe said with a chuckle.

"She really is," Liza said. I honestly didn't care what we had. Boy or girl, as long as it was a healthy child.

Dr. Monroe moved the wand on Liza's stomach as we watched the baby move. "Are you ready to find out the sex?" he asked.

Nodding, I looked down at Liza who was staring at the screen, smiling.

"Yep," I said. "I'm ready. Bring it on, Dr. Monroe."

Reaching for Liza's hand, I held onto it as Dr. Monroe started typing on the screen. *It's a healthy baby boy.*

Liza let out a sob and squeezed my hand. I didn't care that I was being a pussy. I cried. I cried like a damn fool.

Liza wiped her tears away and looked into my eyes as she whispered. "Nickolas Jacob Moore." We had picked our fathers' middle names for our son's name.

I nodded, unable to find the words to speak. *A son.* We were having a son. I was going to teach him everything I knew, just like my father had taught me. Fishing, hunting, the ranching business. How to smile at girls and make their hearts melt and, more importantly, to treat girls with the upmost respect. I closed my eyes, thanking God for our blessing.

## *Four Months Later – May*

I took a step back and looked at the house. *Our house.*

I'd ended up hiring on some people to help out with building the place. I'd wanted to have it done by the time the baby came. We would stay in my parents' rental in Llano for the first few months, then move here.

I looked up at the sandstone structure. Liza loved the massive front and back covered porches. We both talked about the nights we'd sit out here and watch the storms roll in. I walked up the back steps and into the house. I went into the breakfast area and smiled at the window-lined room. The views were amazing. In the kitchen I ran a hand along the granite countertop. Liza had fallen in love with cooking, so we'd put a commercial-grade oven and a prep sink in the island. I peered into the open living room and admired the massive cedar beams running across the ceiling. A massive sandstone fireplace stood in the corner. I pictured it decorated for Christmas with stockings and garland.

I turned and headed down the hallway. The three rooms on this end would be Nickolas's room, a guest room, and an office for Liza. She was handling more and more of the cattle ranch business and was now doing all the books and payroll. She loved it. She loved working alongside her father, my dad, and me.

Jase had told Liza and me how excited he was to be heading into the family business at the end of the summer. He was almost finished with school and would return home after a few months in Italy. Ava was heading to Paris first and then Italy. My mother and father were fit to be tied. I smiled and shook my head. My baby sister was good at what she did—I was glad she was following her fashion dreams.

After walking through all the rooms I headed back across the house to check out the laundry room. I smiled when I saw the finished product. Liza would be happy with the size—it was big enough to have a table and storage, as well as a deep freezer.

I turned down the hall and made my way upstairs. The only room upstairs was the master bedroom. We'd added the addition above the garage at the last minute when Liza and I had decided we needed a more private master suite. I walked in and looked around. There was a separate sitting area with a huge bench that ran along massive windows at the back wall. The windows were flanked by floor-to-ceiling bookshelves. My mother had moaned when she saw it. I was glad that Liza's love for books had grown from my mother's job as a freelance editor. I remembered Liza and Ava sitting on the floor of my parents' room when they were little, listening as my mother read them stories.

I chuckled at the memory. In the master bedroom, the giant walk-in shower was finished and my dick jumped at the thought of taking Liza against the stone tiles. I turned away and adjusted myself—my damn pants felt two sizes too small now. One last look around at the sunken tub and dual vanities, and I was ready to sign off on everything. Liza was going to be really happy with how it all had turned out.

Heading back downstairs, I turned off the lights. I walked into the baby's room one more time. My mother and Whitley were surprising Liza with the room. They'd been working on it for the last week. Liza had become obsessed with Winnie the Pooh, so the entire room was decorated in a Pooh theme. She was going to cry when she saw it.

I checked my watch. Liza was three days overdue, and pretty miserable. Jessica's trial had been last month and it had worn both of us out. Jessica lost it three times during testimony. She was ruled incompetent to stand trial and sent to a psychiatric hospital. My heart broke for her. I still had no clue what had pushed her so far over the edge.

I headed out to the front porch and locked the house. I took in the view of our property. We'd be living on part of Mimi and Frank's old cattle ranch. Liza's lot and mine combined gave us 2500 acres. I knew I wanted to raise horses on our place. Part of our land butted up against Liza's dad's place. Layton and I had already talked about it, and he thought it was a great idea, since I had a keen eye for horses. I couldn't see doing it right now, though. I loved being a part of what my father and Layton had built. Maybe I'd start slowly buying a few horses here and there. Our parents had given us so many opportunities to do great things, anything was possible.

My phone buzzed and I smiled when I saw a text from Liza.

**Liza**: *Can you come to my office?*

Liza had an office in the main barn, just down from her parents' house. She still went into work twice a week, even though I'd begged her to stop working.

**Me**: *Sure. I'll be there in about ten minutes.*

I walked to my truck, got in, and headed to Liza. As I drove, I thought back to our wedding. It had been just Liza and I along with Ava, Jase, and our parents.

*Liza had wanted a small wedding and she'd wanted to have it on the fishing dock where we had so many wonderful memories. I stood next to my father as my heart beat at an uncontrolled rate. I held my breath when I saw Whitley walk up followed by my mother. They both were breathtaking in flowing emerald dresses. I chuckled when I saw that they both wore cowboy boots.*

*Ava followed my mother. She was dressed in a different style dress, but in the same emerald color. Liza was thrilled that Ava had designed all the dresses, including her wedding dress.*

*Then I saw her. Dressed in white with her long, golden-brown hair piled up on top of her head. Long curls blew in the wind as she walked toward me. She wore a simple white dress that dragged the ground as she walked. Her arm was hooked in Layton's and she smiled when Layton whispered something into her ear. I could see her swollen belly peeking out as she moved closer.*

*Layton stopped just short of me and lifted Liza's veil as he whispered something in her ear, causing her to let out a little sob. I smiled. Liza had not been able to keep her emotions in check during her pregnancy—she even cried while watching commercials. Layton kissed her cheek, then put her hand in mine.*

*"Take care of her, Walker. I've loved her since the day I found out she'd be mine. It's hard for me to share her. Notice I said share?"*

*I nodded and tried not to smile. "Yes, sir. I noticed that."*

*He winked. "Good, because she'll always be my little girl. I'm trusting you to always make her smile and to show her every chance you get how much you love her."*

*I wiped the tear from my eye and cursed myself for letting my emotions get to me. I nodded and took Liza's hand and kissed it. I looked into her beautiful blue eyes. "I'll love her with every ounce of my being sir. Forever."*

Walking into the barn, I heard a few people talking. I was pretty sure I heard Whitley and my father. Layton had gone into Austin today for some board meeting for a company he'd invested in. I laughed to myself, knowing how much he hated that kind of stuff. I rounded the corner and saw Whitley and my father standing over Liza, who was sitting in her chair. She was breathing funny. My heart stopped. Everyone looked at me. Whitley smiled sweetly, my father plastered on an "everything is okay" look, and Liza appeared to be doing breathing exercises. *Oh shit. She's in labor*

I dragged in a deep breath. *Stay calm Walker. You won't be one of those guys who freaks out. You're going to be strong for your wife.*

"Hey there," Whitley said, trying to sound calm.

I smiled. "Liza? What's going on?"

Liza smiled that beautiful smile as she stood up. I looked down and her pants where wet. "Walker, we need to get to the hospital. My water broke."

My mouth went dry. "Wh—what?" I said, trying to remind myself to be calm.

She came closer and bit her lip, smiling bigger. "Nickolas is on his way."

Everything in the room spun. I felt my legs start to give out. I dragged in a deep breath. I had no idea how I was staying calm, but I was. I clapped my hands and said, "All right. Let's get this party started. Liza, baby, I've got your bag already in your 4Runner, so let's get you in there and get to the hospital, shall we?"

My father's jaw dropped and Whitley smiled like I was the best thing since apple pie.

Liza's eyes filled with tears. "Thank you for being so calm. I'm so scared."

I pulled her into my arms, holding her for a good minute before I picked her up and carried her to her car.

"I'm here, baby. I'm here and I promise not to leave your side," I whispered.

She buried her face in my chest and let out a small sob. My heart slammed. I wanted nothing more than to freak the fuck out, but I knew I had to be strong for Liza.

My father laughed as Liza squeezed the hell out of my hand, making me bend over in pain, squealing.

"Liza, honey could you let off a little?" I asked.

She snapped her head over and glared at me. Narrowing her eyes, Liza asked, "What? What did you ask?"

Swallowing hard I said, "Nothing. Baby, you squeeze as hard as you need. I'm here for you."

She rolled her eyes and breathed rhythmically. I glanced up at my father. He drove while I sat in the back with Liza on the way to the hospital. Whitley was in the passenger seat and had texted everyone, letting them know Liza was in labor. Jase and Ava came home yesterday from college and were leaving in three days for Europe. I knew Liza was hoping to have the baby before they left.

"How...much...longer?" Liza panted. I pushed her hair back and kissed her.

I looked out the window as my father made a turn and. "We're here, baby girl. We're here," he said, as he pulled up to the front entrance of the hospital. I jumped out and ran in, skidding to a stop when I came to the front desk.

There was an older lady sitting there. Her silver hear was pulled back tight. She smiled at me sweetly. "May I help you, sir?"

"My wife is in labor. She's..." I turned and pointed. My dad and Whitley were helping Liza out of the 4Runner. "She's getting out of the car now."

Turning back to the older lady I saw that she was already walking past me with a wheelchair. "Well, let's go get her."

I followed her, trying to stay calm. "Her water broke," I blurted.

She nodded and smiled. "Did you call her doctor?"

I stopped walking. *Fuck.*

"Keep walking and wipe that look of horror from your face, son," she said as the door opened and she headed outside. "Well hello there darling," she said to Liza. "My name is Nancy. I'm going to help you get to labor and delivery."

Liza gave the woman a weak smile. "Hello, Nancy."

Sitting in the wheelchair, Liza reached for my hand. I quickly gave it to her, just in time for another contraction. This time she almost brought me to my knees with how hard she squeezed. I looked at my father who was laughing his ass off. I narrowed my eyes at him and whispered, "She's gonna break my hand!"

"She probably will!" He started laughing again.

Nancy began to head over to the elevator. "Sweetheart what's your name?" Nancy asked Liza as we waited for the elevator.

"L—Liza,"

"Liza, did you call your doctor?" Nancy asked as she looked at me and winked.

Liza nodded and Whitley said, "Yes. As soon as her water broke, she called."

I let out the breath I'd been holding.

The elevator ride to the labor and delivery floor felt like an eternity. When the doors opened, we all stepped out. Nancy pushed Liza to the nurse's desk and gave them her name. They asked all kinds of questions.

Insurance, how far apart the contractions were, how far along she was—my head was spinning. Before long, we were in a delivery room that would also serve as Liza and the baby's room afterward.

I'd forgotten how beautiful their rooms were. Liza and I had toured the hospital's labor and delivery floor a few months back. The walls were a soft green and the dark walnut cabinets flanking the hospital bed looked brand new. I knew they'd remodeled a lot of the rooms, but this was like a five-star hotel. There was a sofa up against the windows with a dark, walnut rocking chair next to it. The wall of windows looked out over the hill country and the view was amazing. To the left of the bed was a Jacuzzi tub.

"Damn," I whispered as walked toward the bed. They were getting Liza out of her clothes and into a hospital gown when a contraction hit her.

"Walker!" she cried as I quickly moved to the side of the bed, out of the nurse's way.

"I'm right here, baby. I'm right here." I took her hand and talked her through the contraction.

We got Liza settled and into the bed as the nurses hooked her up to a bunch of machines. She was so strong, breathing through each contraction. I was so proud of her. Leaning over I gave her a gentle kiss. She opened her eyes and smiled.

"I love you so much and I'm so proud of you, Liza. I'll never be able to put into words how much I love you. How happy you've made me." My eyes searched her face before our blue eyes locked. "You're so beautiful. I've never seen you more beautiful."

The tear that rolled down her face caused a lump in my throat. "Breathtakingly beautiful," I whispered as I captured her lips with mine.

She pulled me in closer as we deepened the kiss. Eventually, the nurse cleared her throat. I pulled back and whispered against her lips. "I love you, baby."

She smiled and wiped away her tear. "I love you, too."

It wasn't long before the sounds of our baby boy's cries filled the air. Liza had been amazing and only had to push for thirty minutes before Nickolas made his appearance. I sat next to her as she held Nickolas in her arms. She looked at me and smiled.

"I've never been so happy in my entire life," she said, her eyes bright with love.

I caressed our son's cheek with my finger. "The two most important people in my life," I whispered as I kissed Nickolas's head and then Liza's lips.

Nickolas whimpered and Liza laughed. I pulled back and looked down at my little guy. "All from a promise," I said.

Liza and I looked into each other's eyes. A tear rolled down Liza's face as she said, "A promise of love."

# Twenty-Nine

## Liza
*Two Months Later*

Sitting in the living room I tried to concentrate on work and I couldn't. I stood up and stretched, looking at all the boxes everywhere. I rolled my eyes and went to the kitchen to grab a bottle of water. I leaned back against the counter and smiled. I could hear Walker talking to Nickolas over the baby monitor. I loved listening to him talk to Nickolas. Pushing off the counter, I headed upstairs to Nickolas's room.

Walker hummed as he walked around the room, holding Nickolas close to his bare chest, lulling him to sleep. I leaned against the wall, watching my two favorite men. Seeing the two of them together made my heart burst with happiness. I loved them both so much. Walker was an amazing dad. From the time we brought Nickolas home, he was hands-on. My favorite time was bath time, all three of us together. Walker would wrap Nickolas up in a towel and bring him to our room. He'd place the baby between us and we'd lie there, talking. Nickolas seemed to take it all in. It was our time. I imagined doing it as the years went by. The older Nickolas got, the more the conversations would grow.

"Are you ready to move into your new home, little man?" Walker said. "I can't wait for you to see your new room. If you think this is nice, you haven't seen anything yet!"

I giggled and shook my head. Our moms had done an amazing job on Nickolas's room at the new house. It was everything Winnie the Pooh, and I loved it. We'd planned on staying here longer, but I wanted to get back to work and I hated being in town, away from our families. I'd talked to Walker a few weeks ago about moving into our new home. It was ready to go, and it made sense to move in and get settled. Nickolas was two months old, and I thought the transition would be easier now than when he got older.

My phone buzzed in my back pocket. It was a text from Jase. He was heading home in a few days. He'd stayed in Europe longer then he'd originally planned. Of course the girl he'd met had played a hand in that, I'm sure. I loved that her name was Taylor, too.

**Jase**: *How is my nephew doing?*
**Me**: *Wonderfully. He's in one of his favorite places—Daddy's arms.*
**Jase**: *I can't wait to see him. I miss home. Miss the ranch*

Jase had been struggling with something and I couldn't put my finger on it.

**Me**: *Home has missed you. How's Ava?*
**Jase**: *Ava's good. Liza, I really need to talk when I get home.*
**Me**: *Is everything okay?*
**Jase**: *Yeah, just feeling confused. Gotta run. Love you.*
**Me**: *Love you, too. We'll talk soon.*

I felt him before I saw him. Walker stood in front of me with the goofiest smile on his face. I cocked my head at him. "What's with the smile?"

I glanced behind him and saw Nickolas was sound asleep in his crib. I looked back and was immediately lost in Walker's eyes.

"*You* make me smile. You make my heart feel like it could burst at any moment. You're so beautiful, Liza. I have to catch my breath when you walk into a room."

Taking his hand in mine, I pulled Walker out of Nickolas's room and down the hall to our room. I glanced at the double heart ring, still on my finger. My heart skipped a beat.

Entering the room, Walker shut the door behind him. He leaned against it and gave me that smile that made my stomach flutter with a million butterflies.

"Do you remember that day in the barn?" I asked as my eyes searched his.

His eyes lit up with passion. "The first time we ever kissed? I could never forget that day, Liza."

I spun the ring on my finger as I gazed into his eyes. I was taken back to that one moment. The moment I promised to wait for him. The moment I promised to myself that he would have my heart forever. One promise I had broken. The other promise I would keep until I'd taken my last breath.

Walker pushed his body right up against mine. He placed his lips next to my ear. "You walk into a room and my heart stops."

I gasped as he covered my neck with soft kisses. Pulling back some, he looked at me with nothing put love in his eyes. My heart raced. I was sure Walker could hear it.

Walker cupped my face with his hands. His thumbs gently traced over my skin eliciting goose bumps all over my body. "Your love takes my breath away, Liza."

I moaned as he pressed his lips to mine. As always, we were lost in each other the moment our lips made contact. Every movement of our tongues, every moan, and every bare-skinned touch—we were lost in a world where we were one. Lost in our love.

Walker was my everything, and I was his everything. We were a promise, made to each other. A promise that would be bound by something so strong it could never break.

A promise bound by love.

Forever.

# Epilogue

## Walker

I sat on the steps of the back porch of our house and watched Liza play with Nickolas. His birthday party was winding down and everyone had finally gone home. Liza glanced over to me and smiled. "I think he's ready for a nap!" She called out.

Nodding, I said, "I give him two minutes."

Liza was walking with Nickolas back up to the porch. Nickolas stopped in front of me and grinned. I smiled back and held my hands out for him. I lifted him up as I stood and the three of us made our way into the house.

"I'm Fwee, Daddy!" Nickolas said with a smile and then a yawn.

I patted his back and he rested his head on my chest. "I know buddy. You're a big boy now, but big boys need naps, too."

Liza pulled the covers back and I placed Nickolas into his toddler bed. He didn't even do the normal routine where he tried to stay up as long as possible. He pulled his covers up and shut his eyes, holding his stuffed Pooh Bear. I peeked over to Liza. She made a funny face and giggled.

Tip-toeing out of his room, I shut the door and started down the hall. "Should we clean up now or wait until later? I think I'm ready for a nap."

Liza flashed me a sexy grin. She started for our room upstairs and I followed. *Oh man. A nap is going to feel so good.*

"I can't wait for my head to hit the pillow," I said as I followed Liza up the stairs.

We walked into the room and I quickly pulled off my T-shirt and sat on the bed.

Liza came over to me and sat on my lap, wrapping her legs around me. She leaned down and brushed her lips against mine. "I have something I have to tell you," she whispered against my lips.

I looked into her blue eyes and smiled. "I'm all ears, darlin'."

She bit her lip. I chuckled as I pulled it from her teeth. Then she smiled the most breath-taking smile. I felt like all the air was pulled from my lungs as I watched that smile spread across her face, her eyes so bright they could have been seen from across the room.

She placed her hands on my face and brushed her thumbs across my lips.

"I'm pregnant."

My heart slammed in my chest and my stomach dropped. I was sure the smile on my face matched hers.

"We're having another baby?" I asked as tears formed in my eyes.

She nodded and winked. "And this time, I'm *positive* it's a girl. I just feel it."

I laughed as I looked at my beautiful wife. I thought my life had been complete up until this very moment. We hadn't talked about any more kids. If it happened, it happened. My heart beat like crazy at the idea of another baby. We were going to give Nickolas a baby brother or sister.

Placing my hand on her stomach, I looked into her eyes. "Our love is forever, Liza," I whispered.

She placed her hand over mine. "Love me, Walker."

I pulled her body closer and placed my lips against hers. "Always."


The End

Look for Ava's story in…

# Broken Love

Available now at your favorite ebook retailer.

# Thank You

To my readers/friends, none of this would be possible without y'all. Every day I wake up, I smile, knowing that at least a few of y'all are going to make my day with a note, a funny post, a comment to tell me that you recommended the book to someone, or just a simple, *Hey*. Thank you for your support and for your love of these characters. They are so very dear to my heart, and it is a privilege that I'm able to share them with y'all. I hope you get lost in their world just as much as I do.

Darrin, I just don't even know what to say. You are my rock—my true love who has always been by my side since the very beginning. I love you so much, and I can't thank you enough for your support in all of this. Even when it takes me away from you so much, you still support it, and that makes me love you even more.

Now, on to bigger things—yes, yes, I know when you read the books that some things seem *very familiar*. Get over it, babe. I'm always going to use what you do and say and put them into my books. Think of it as memories forever frozen in time! Besides, you give me SO much material that I feel like it's my duty to share it with the world. I love you, and I'll love you forever, Darrin.

Laure, you are growing up before my eyes. Please stop. It makes me so sad, and not to mention, it makes me feel old. You make me laugh, and sometimes you make me want to scream when you roll your eyes at me. I don't know where you got that from (rolling my eyes as I type that).

You are becoming such an amazing young woman, Lauren. Always stay true to yourself and know that there is nothing in this world you can't do if you want it bad enough. Believe in yourself and your dreams always. I love doo!

Mom, I miss you so much. I hope that I've made you proud of the person I strive to be each and every day. Love you, Mom.

# *Playlist*

Keith Urban – "We Were Us"
*Walker and Liza seeing each other for the first time after college.*

Florida Georgia Line – "This Is How We Roll"
*Dancing at Luckenbach Dance Hall.*

Thompson Square – "Glass"
*Liza and Walker dancing at Luckenback Dance Hall.*

Blake Shelton – "Who Are You When I'm Not Looking"
*Liza and Walker dancing at Luckenback Dance Hall.*

Brantley Gilbert – "Fall Into Me"
*Liza and Walker almost kissing at the bed and breakfast.*

Hunter Hayes – "Story Line"
*Liza and Walker dancing at distillery party.*

Jessie Ware – "Say You Love Me"
*Walker almost kisses Liza while dancing at distillery party.*

Ariana Grande – "Just A Little Bit Of Your Love"
*Liza walking up to the hunters cabin to talk to Walker.*

Lady Antebellum – "I Did With You"
*Liza and Walker making love for the first time.*

Miranda Lambert – "Holding On To You"
*Walker holding Liza after they make love.*

Kris Allen – "Leave You Alone"
*Walker pushing Liza away after the accident.*

Chase Rice – "Gonna Wanna Tonight"
*Liza and Walker during their date night in Austin.*

George Straight – "Love Is Everything"
*Walker and Liza dancing during their date night in Austin.*

Brad Paisley – "Perfect Storm"
*Liza getting Walker back on a horse. Then telling him she is pregnant.*

Keith Urban – "Once In A Lifetime"
*Liza giving birth and the epilogue.*

The complete playlist of songs I used while
writing this book can be found on my website.

# Other Titles

**Wanted Series**

*Wanted*
*Saved*
*Faithfu*
*Believe*
*Cherished*
*A Forever Love*
*The Wanted Short Stories*
*All They Wanted*

Entire series on Audiobook

**Love Wanted in Texas Series (Wanted spin off series)**

*Without You*
*Saving You*
*Holding You*
*Finding You*
*Chasing You*
*Loving You*

Entire series on Audiobook

## Broken Series

*Broken*
*Broken Dreams*
*Broken Promises*
*Broken Love*

First three books on Audiobook

## Journey of Love Series

*Unconditional Love*
*Undeniable Love*
*Unforgettable Love*

Entire series on Audiobook

## Speed Series

*Ignite*
*Adrenaline*

## With Me Series

*Stay With Me*
*Only With Me* (coming 1.31.17)

## Boston Love Series

*Searching For Harmony*
*Fighting for Love* (coming 4.4.17)

## Stand Alones

*The Journey Home*
*Who We Were* (Available on audio book)
*The Playbook* (Available on Audiobook
*Made for You*

# Coming Soon

## Fated Hearts Series

*Heart in Motion* (Coming 6.27.17)
*Guarded Hearts* (Coming 7.25.17)

## Seduced Series

*Seduced* (Coming 9.12.17)

## Joint Projects

*Finding Forever* (Co-written with Kristin Mayer)
*Stories for Amanda*

## Young Adult – writing as Ella Bordeaux

*Beautiful*
*Forever Beautiful* (coming March 2017

CPSIA information can be obtained
at www.ICGtesting.com
Printed in the USA
BVHW041821080620
581125BV00013B/467